Ro

STOP THE PRESS—*Crown Prince in shock marriage*

The tabloid headlines…

When Crown Prince Alessandro of Santina proposes to paparazzi favorite Allegra Jackson, it promises to be *the* social event of the decade…

Outrageous headlines guaranteed!

The salacious gossip…

Harlequin Presents® invites you to rub shoulders with royalty, sheikhs and glamorous socialites. Step into the decadent playground of the world's rich and famous, where… *one thing is for sure—royalty has never been so scandalous!*

Beginning May 2012

THE PRICE OF ROYAL DUTY—Penny Jordan

THE SHEIKH'S HEIR—Sharon Kendrick

SANTINA'S SCANDALOUS PRINCESS—Kate Hewitt

THE MAN BEHIND THE SCARS—Caitlin Crews

DEFYING THE PRINCE—Sarah Morgan

PRINCESS FROM THE SHADOWS—Maisey Yates

THE GIRL NOBODY WANTED—Lynn Raye Harris

PLAYING THE ROYAL GAME—Carol Marinelli

"Do you want to be my fiancée?"

"Alex," Allegra said, "why when I didn't even want to have a drink with you do you think I'd even entertain….?"

"A million pounds."

She laughed, because these things didn't happen and he had to be joking, and when he pulled out a checkbook, she laughed even more, because it was crazy. Except when he handed it to her, his hand was completely steady and he wasn't laughing.

"You might not have to do anything. I will fly to Santina tomorrow and tell my family. The people will be outraged— soon enough I'll be told to reverse my foolish decision, to come back to London till the scandal dies down…."

"So what are you paying me for?"

"I can't just invent someone—you might have to join me in Santina at some point. All you would have to do is smile and hang on my every word."

"Until?"

"Until the people dictate otherwise." He gave a shrug. "It might be days, it might be weeks." He looked to the check and so, too, did Allegra, and she thought about it—hell, she really thought about it. He wasn't asking for her to sleep with him—just to smile and hold his hand. And what she could do with the money… She could get a flat, a job. Actually she could do what she really wanted…

"You could finally write that book." It was as if he had stepped into her mind. She heard his voice as if he was inside it, but it was madness, it couldn't work….

"Is that a yes?" Alex asked and she looked back at him, thought not just of the book she could write but of a link to this man, this beautiful man who had entered her life—and somehow she simply wasn't quite ready to let go of him.

Carol Marinelli

PLAYING THE ROYAL GAME

HARLEQUIN®

entertain, enrich, inspire™

Recycling programs
for this product may
not exist in your area.

ISBN-13: 978-0-373-13108-2

PLAYING THE ROYAL GAME

Copyright © 2012 by Harlequin Books S.A.

Special thanks and acknowledgment are given to Carol Marinelli for her contribution to The Santina Crown series.

www.Harlequin.com

Printed in U.S.A.

All about the author…
Carol Marinelli

CAROL MARINELLI finds writing a bio rather like writing her New Year's resolutions. Oh, she'd love to say that since she wrote the last one, she now goes to the gym regularly and doesn't stop for coffee and cake and a gossip afterward; that she's incredibly organized and writes for a few productive hours a day after tidying her immaculate house and taking a brisk walk with the dog.

The reality is that Carol spends an inordinate amount of time daydreaming about dark, brooding men and exotic places (research), which doesn't leave too much time for the gym, housework or anything that comes in between, and her most productive writing hours happen to be in the middle of the night, which leaves her in a constant state of bewildered exhaustion.

Originally from England, Carol now lives in Melbourne, Australia. She adores going back to the U.K. for a visit—actually, she adores going anywhere for a visit—and constantly (expensively) strives to overcome her fear of flying. She has three gorgeous children who are growing up so fast (too fast—they've just worked out that she lies about her age!) and keep her busy with a never-ending round of homework, sport and friends coming over.

A nurse and a writer, Carol writes for the Harlequin Presents® and Medical Romance lines and is passionate about both. She loves the fast-paced, busy setting of a modern hospital, but every now and then admits it's bliss to escape to the glamorous, alluring world of her Presents heroes and heroines. A bit like her real life, actually!

Other titles by Carol Marinelli available in eBook:

Harlequin Presents®

3047—A SHAMEFUL CONSEQUENCE *(The Secrets of Xanos)*
3053—AN INDECENT PROPOSITION *(The Secrets of Xanos)*
3097—BANISHED TO THE HAREM *(Empire of the Sands)*

CHAPTER ONE

SHE was better off without the job, Allegra told herself.

No one should have to put up with that.

Except that walking in the rain along grey London streets, taking the underground to various employment agencies, the anger that her boss could make such a blatant a pass at her and then fire her for not succumbing started to be replaced with something that felt close to fear.

She needed that job.

Needed it.

Her savings had been obliterated by the bottomless pit that was her family's excess spending. At times it felt as if her lowly publishing wage supported half the Jackson family. Yes, she was the boring reliable one, but they didn't mind her dependability when their erratic ways found them in trouble. Just last week she had lent her step-mother, Chantelle, close to five thousand pounds in cash for credit card debts that her father didn't know about. It was laughable to think that she might now have to have her family support her.

It was a miserable day, with no sign that it was spring; instead it was cold and wet, and Allegra dug her hands deeper into her trench coat pockets, her fingers curling around a fifty-pound note she had pulled out of the ATM.

If her boss refused to put her pay in tomorrow it was all she had before being completely broke.

No!

She'd been through worse than this, Allegra decided. As Bobby Jackson's daughter she was all too used to the bailiffs but her father always managed to pick himself up; he never let it get him down. She was not going to sink, but hell, if she did, then she'd sink in style!

Pushing open a bar door, she walked in with her head held high, the heat hitting her as she entered, and Allegra slipped off her coat and hung it, her hair dripping wet and cold down her back. Normally she wouldn't entertain entering some random bar, but still, at least it was warm and she could sit down and finally gather her thoughts.

There had been a confidence to her as she'd stalked out of her office with dignity. With her track record and her job history, a lot of the agencies had called over the years offering her freelance work.

It had been sobering indeed to find out that they were hiring no one, that the financial crisis and changes to the industry meant that there were no causal jobs waiting for her to step into.

None.

Well, a chance for a couple, but they added up to about three hours' work per month.

Per month!

Allegra was about to head to the bar but, glancing around, saw that it was table service so she walked over to a small alcove and took a seat, the plush couch lined with velvet. Despite its rather dingy appearance from the street, inside it was actually very nice and the prices on the menu verified that as fact.

She looked up at the sound of laughter—a group of well-dressed women were sipping on cocktails and Allegra couldn't help but envy their buoyant mood. As her eyes moved away from the jovial women they stilled for a fraction, because there, sitting at a table near them, lost in his own world, was possibly the most beautiful man ever to come into her line of vision. Dark suited, his thick brown hair was raked back to show an immaculate profile, high cheekbones and a very straight nose; his long legs were stretched out and crossed at the ankle. But despite his rather languorous position, as he stared into his glass there was a pensiveness to him, a furrow between his eyebrows that showed he was deep in thought. The furrow deepened as there was another outbreak of laughter from the women's table, and just as he looked up, just as he might have caught her watching, Allegra was terribly grateful for the distraction of the waitress who approached.

'What can I get you?' Allegra was about to order a glass of house wine, or maybe just ask if they could do her a pot of tea and a sandwich, because she really ought to try a couple more job agencies, but hell, a girl could only take so much rejection in one day and she may well be living off tea and sandwiches for a long while yet!

'A bottle of Bollinger please.' It was an extravagant gesture for Allegra, an unusual one as well. She was extremely careful with her pay cheque, saving twenty percent to put towards her first mortgage before it even hit her account, determined never to be like her family—but where had that gotten her?

The waitress didn't bat an eye; instead she asked how many glasses.

'Just the one.'

She was given a little bowl of nuts too!

'Celebrating?' the waitress asked as she poured her drink.

'Sort of,' Allegra admitted, and then, left alone, she

decided that she was. For months she had put up with her boss's thinly veiled leers and skin-crawling comments. It was worth celebrating just to finally be past all that, so she raised her glass to the window, in the general direction of her old work place.

'Cheers!'

As she turned she caught Mr. Gorgeous watching her— not staring, just idly curious—and she couldn't blame him for that. After all, she was raising a glass to the window. She gave him a brief smile and then turned back to her thoughts, took out a pen and the notebook and list of contacts that she always carried and set about making copious lists, determined, *determined*, that by the end of the week she would be back in work.

Halfway down the bottle and she didn't feel quite so brave. If anything, half a bottle of champagne on an empty stomach had her emotions bubbling and she was dangerously close to tears, especially when the waitress came over.

'You didn't sign the register when you came in,' the waitress said, and even before she continued Allegra knew what was coming and inwardly flinched as realization dawned. 'You are a member, aren't you?' She felt a blush spread on her cheeks. Of course it was a private club that she'd entered, not some bar she'd just wandered into, and just as she was about to apologise and fling down her fifty-pound note and flee, a voice that was as pleasing as its owner saved her the embarrassment.

'Why are you hiding there?' A deep warm voice had both Allegra and the waitress turn around and she found herself looking now into the eyes of the pensive stranger— very brown eyes that stayed steady as hers blinked in confusion. He turned and addressed the waitress. 'Sorry, she's my guest. I'll sign her in in a moment.' The waitress opened her mouth to say something—after all, Allegra had been sitting there alone for a good half an hour or so and he had made no effort to join his *guest*—but perhaps he was a favourite customer, or maybe it was just his impressive stance, because, without comment, the waitress left them to it.

'Thanks,' Allegra said as he took a seat in front of her. 'But no thanks. I'll just settle my bill....' She went to go, but as he moved to stop her, his hand reaching across the table, she shot him a look that told him unwelcome contact would be a *very* foolish mistake on his part. Given the day she'd had, Allegra had enough pent-up energy to give this stranger a little piece of her mind.

'As I said, thank you, but no thank you.'

'At least finish your drink,' said the stranger. 'It would be a shame to waste it.'

It would be a crying shame actually.

Maybe she could take it with her, Allegra thought wildly, having visions of herself walking down the street, half-drunk bottle in hand, bemoaning her situation. She found herself smiling at the very thought—not smiling at him, of course, except he interpreted it as such, because he clicked slender fingers in the direction of the bar and summoned another glass. Allegra sat bristling as the waitress poured him a glass of *her* champagne.

'I'm just trying to enjoy a quiet drink alone,' she said pointedly.

'Then sign in,' he suggested.

'Ha, ha!'

'Or,' he offered, 'you can be my guest, which means you sit with me. I wouldn't hear of it otherwise.' She couldn't place his accent. He spoke English terribly well; in fact, his voice was clipped and well schooled, unlike Allegra's rather more London accent, but there was a slight ring to it, Spanish or Italian perhaps. She was determined not to stay long enough to find out.

'Anyway,' he carried on despite her lack of response, 'you don't look as if you are enjoying it. In fact, apart from the small salute to the window you seem as miserable as I am.' She looked at him and saw that the impressive suit he was wearing wasn't just dark, it was black, and so, too, the tie. Not just from the attire, but from the strain on his face, he had clearly come from a funeral. Now he was close, she could smell him—and he smelt nothing like the usual man in a bar. It wasn't just the delicious hint of cologne that was unusual; he actually smelt of clean—there was no other way to describe it. His eyes were clear and bizarrely she felt herself relax just a little, for this was surely not a man who usually pressed attention, and it wasn't as if she had anywhere else that she needed to be.

'Are you usually so invasive?'

He thought about it for a moment. 'No.' He took a sip of drink and seemed to think about it some more. 'Never. I just saw you looking so fed up and then when the waitress came over I thought…'

'That you'd cheer me up?'

'No.' He gave a small shrug. 'I thought we could be miserable together. Don't look, but there are a group of women…' He gestured his head and as instructed she didn't look, but she knew who he meant. She'd heard their flirting laughter, and had easily guessed it was aimed towards him. 'One of them in particular seems determined to join me.'

'I'd have thought you'd have no trouble at all fighting off unwelcome attention.' Unlike me, she didn't add, but then she wasn't particularly used to men vying for her attention—well, not gorgeous ones anyway. But knowing how to deflect unwelcome attention was surely a prerequisite to him stepping out on the street, because wherever he went he surely turned heads.

'Normally, I have no problem.' He didn't say it in arrogance, merely stated the fact. 'Just today.' She looked at his suit. 'I was just trying to have a drink, to think, to have some silence, perhaps the same as you....' And while she'd have chosen to have some peace, she'd settle for silence too.

'Okay.' She gave a begrudging smile. 'I can manage silence.'

He must be someone, because all she had been given was a small bowl of nuts, but now that he'd joined her she was treated to lots of little bowls of goodies. She didn't care if she looked greedy; the rumble in her stomach reminded Allegra that she hadn't eaten since the slice of toast she'd had while dashing to the Underground some seven hours ago.

'I'd better sign you in,' he said. 'I'm surprised you got to a table. They are normally very...' He didn't finish, but the insinuation that she didn't belong had her blushing to her roots.

'Particular!' Allegra finished for him, and again she went to reach for her bag. She did not need his charity and certainly not his insults. Today really wasn't proving to be the best.

'Thorough.' He actually smiled at her indignation, a lovely smile that suited him—the very first smile from him that she had seen—and it changed him, changed those haughty, guarded features in a way she rather liked. It was a small smile, not a wide one, a smile she somehow knew was one that was rarely shared. It had to be rare, she figured, because the effect was completely devastating. It fostered awareness, made even listening somehow terribly difficult, because what had offended just a moment before hardly mattered a jot as he spoke on. She had to remind herself that a few seconds ago she'd been rather disgruntled, had to force herself to not sit there like an idiot and smile back. 'I meant that they are usually very thorough.'

'You're forgiven then.' And despite her best intentions, Allegra realised she was smiling back.

'What's your name?'

'Allegra,' she said. 'Allegra Jackson. Two *l*'s.'

'I'm Aless…' He hesitated, just for a second. 'Alex.'

And she watched as he headed off, breathed a little sigh of relief, because normally when she said her name there was a frown, or a little flare of recognition. Her family managed to hit the newsstands with alarming regularity, and even though she was, in the main, left out of the scandal and gossip they all generated, her rather unusual first name, combined with the surname of Jackson generally led to the inevitable… 'Are you Bobby Jackson's daughter?'

He headed over to the book and signed her in in the guest column. He'd almost given his real name. It wasn't exactly a secret but in general, and especially in London, he went by Alex Santina, businessman extraordinaire, not HRH Crown Prince Alessandro Santina. He guessed the slip-up was because he'd been sitting there thinking about Santina, thinking about the angry discussion he'd recently had with his father. He was tired too, Alex realised, and that was unusual, for fatigue was a rare visitor for him. But lately he'd felt it, and today, standing in that church, it had washed over him and literally drained him. He did not recognise that he was upset; funerals did not upset him and he had attended many. He'd hardly known Charles after all.

He signed Allegra in and then walked back towards her. He'd seen her arrive and could fully understand the waitress's mistake—often the doors opened and before they were questioned as to their membership people would shrink back, realising their mistake. But she, or rather Allegra, after a brief glance around, had taken off her coat and hung it up. There was a quiet confidence to her, an ease in her surroundings that would, Alex knew, have had the waitress assume she was a member.

He took his seat and then changed his mind and stood to take off his jacket, the waitress practically tripping over herself to catch it.

He didn't smile at the waitress, Allegra noticed, nor did he thank her.

Nor did he glance over to the table of women who had fallen rather silent as he peeled off the black garment to reveal a crisp white shirt that set off his olive skin. There were no horrible surprises beneath his jacket, just a toe-curling moment as he tucked his shirt in a little, and Allegra again breathed in the scent of him, wanted another glimpse of that smile. But it had retreated now and he gave her the silence she'd insisted on and just sat and stared beyond her and out of the window, his index finger idly circling the top of the glass. Maybe it was too much champagne, or maybe he knew exactly what he was doing, maybe he had a doctorate in suggestive flirting, because for a bizarre moment she wished she were beneath his finger, wished it was her that he idly stroked.

'Sorry.' He misinterpreted her shifting in discomfort. 'I'm not much company—today has been a harder one than I expected.'

'Was it someone close?' she asked, for it was clear he had been to a funeral.

'Not really.' He thought for a moment. 'He works for me, or rather he did—Charles. We were, in fact, here last week for his retirement.' He glanced around the room clearly remembering.

'I'm sorry.'

'For what?'

'That's just what you say, isn't it,' Allegra responded, wishing he wouldn't make her cheeks burn so, wishing he didn't make her over-think every last word.

'He wasn't a friend,' Alex said, and topped up his champagne. 'Really, I hardly knew him—you don't have to be sorry.'

'Then I'm not!' She blew up her fringe with her breath, gorgeous to look at he may be, but he really was rather hard work. 'I'm not in the least sorry that you've been to a funeral and that you're feeling a bit low. Funerals do that…' she added. 'Even if you hardly know the person.'

'They don't bother me,' Alex said. 'And believe me, I've been to many.' And then he conceded. 'Well, usually they don't get to me.'

She wasn't going to risk saying sorry again.

'So what's your excuse?' He looked up from his glass. 'Or do you regularly sit nursing a bottle of champagne in the afternoon.'

She actually laughed. 'Er, no. I lost my job.' He didn't fill the silence, he didn't offer condolences as anyone else would; he just sat until it was Allegra who spoke on. 'Or rather I just walked out.'

'Can I ask why?'

She hesitated, and then gave a tight shrug. 'My boss, he…' The blush on her cheeks said it all.

'Not in your job description?' Alex said, and she was relieved that he got it. 'There are avenues for you…tribunals.'

'I don't want to go down that route,' Allegra said. 'I don't want…' She didn't finish what she was saying, not quite comfortable to reveal who her family was, so she moved on without elaborating. 'I thought I'd easily get another. It would seem I was wrong. Things really are tough out there.'

'Very tough,' Alex said, and though she had been looking at him, she flicked her eyes away, bit down a smart retort, for what would a man like him know about tough times?

'I'm very conscious of my responsibility,' Alex explained, something she had never really considered. 'If I screw up…' She felt the tension in her jaw seep out just a little. 'I employ a lot of people.' He did what for him was unusual, yet he did not hesitate; he went into his jacket and handed her his card.

'You just found another job.'

She looked at the name—Santina Financiers—and of course she knew who he was then: Alex Santina. His companies seemed to ride the wave of financial crisis with ease. He was all over the business magazines, and… She screwed up her forehead, trying to place him further, for she had read about him elsewhere, but half a bottle of Bollinger on a very empty stomach didn't aide instant recall.

She looked at the card and then back to him, to liquid brown eyes and the smile that was, frankly, dangerous. There was a confidence to him, an air of certainty—and she knew in that moment why he was so completely successful. There was an absence of fear to him; there was no other way she could describe it. 'You don't even know what I do for a living.'

His mind was constantly busy and he tried to hazard a guess. He doubted fashion—he'd seen the sensible tweed trousers that were beneath the table. And it wasn't makeup—she wasn't wearing a scrap. He could see the teeny indent at the bridge of her nose from glasses….

'Schoolteacher perhaps?' Alex mused, and he saw her pale neck lengthen as she threw her head back and laughed. 'Librarian…' She shook her head. 'Let me guess,' he said.

Was it ridiculous that he was vaguely turned on as he tried
to fathom her? He looked into eyes that were very green, a
rare green that took him to a place he hadn't been in ages,
to long horse rides in Santina, right into the hills and the
shaded woods, to the moss he would like to lie her down
on. No, he wasn't just vaguely turned on; he saw the dila-
tion of her pupils, like a black full moon rising, and maybe
he knew what she did, because there was comfort there in
her eyes, there was deep knowing too, and he wanted to
stay there. 'Those phone lines—' he moved forward just
a little '—when people don't know what to do...' He saw
her blink, could feel the warmth of her knee as he brushed
against it. 'They ring you?'

'No.' She didn't laugh at this suggestion, she hardly
dared move, because she could feel his leg and wanted
it to stay there, wanted to lean across the table and meet
his mouth, but she snapped herself out of it, pulled back
in her seat and ended whatever strange place he had just
beckoned her to. 'I work in publishing—I'm a copy edi-
tor. Was,' she added. She wanted to signal the waitress,
wanted a glass of water, hell, she'd take the jug and pour
it over herself this second.

'I'm sure I could find you something....'

That really would be out of the frying pan and into the
fire, Allegra thought, offering him back his card with a
shake of her head. But her hand trembled slightly as it did
so, because what a lovely fire it would be to burn in.

'I'll find something.'

'I'm sure you will,' Alex said. 'Keep it. You might
change your mind.'

'Do you normally go around hiring your staff in bars?'

'I leave the hiring to others. If you ring that number
you would only get as far as my assistant, Belinda. I can
tell her to expect—'

'That won't be necessary,' Allegra interrupted. 'I'm just talking, not asking for a solution.'

'It is how my brain works,' Alex admitted. 'Problem—solve it.'

'When sometimes all you have to do is listen.'

She watched as he visibly wrestled with such a suggestion, guessed that this man was not used to sitting idly by in any situation, that he was more than used to coming up with a rapid solution. But as he took another drink and stared out to the bar where he had stood with his colleague last week, perhaps it dawned on him then that not everything came with a solution, and he gave a small nod. 'Charles had many plans for his retirement—he was talking about them last week. I guess it got me thinking.'

Allegra nodded.

'All the things you want to do,' he continued, 'intend to do…cannot do.'

'Cannot?' Allegra asked, because surely a man like Alex could do anything he wanted. He had looks that opened doors, and from his name, from the cut of his hair to the beautifully shod feet, she knew it wasn't his finances that would stop him.

'This time next year…' He was unusually pensive, not that she could know, but now, this afternoon, he felt as if time were running out. 'I'll be married.'

Allegra gave him a very wide-eyed look. 'If you're engaged then you should not be joining women in a bar and sharing a bottle of champagne with them. Shouldn't be…' She halted, not wanting to voice the word, because for a little while there they'd been flirting—not even flirting, far more than that. It had felt as if they had been kissing. She really was going now anyway; *he'd* nearly finished the bottle. And maybe it was an overreaction to leave so hastily, but there was something about him that screamed warning. Not that he was inappropriate, more the wander of her own thoughts, because his mere finger on a glass had had her mind wandering. Something about him told her he'd make it terribly, terribly easy to break very firm rules.

'Don't leave…' As she put down the note his fingers pressed over hers, wrapped them around the bill and held them a fraction. It was first contact and it was blistering; she could feel the heat from his fingers warm not just her own but race, too, to her face. 'I'm not in love…I'm betrothed.'

'There's a difference?' She smarted, though she was curious as to his unusual choice of word. She'd never heard a man, never heard anyone, describe themselves as betrothed. What *was* the difference?

'God, yes.'

Go, her mind told her, just turn around and go! Except his hand was still curled around her fingers and there was sudden torture in the dark eyes that held hers.

'I am Crown Prince Alessandro Santina.' He was too weary to dodge the facts and so rarely wanting of conversation, strangely willing to reveal his truth. 'I have been told I am to return and fulfill my duties.'

She could not have known just how many times she would replay that moment—could never have guessed how often she would look back to the very last time that she could simply have walked away.

She didn't though.

Despite herself, Allegra sat and heard the rest.

CHAPTER TWO

'SHE was chosen for me.'

She knew about arranged marriages, except she was rather surprised to hear that that might be a problem for him. He didn't look like a man who would do anything he didn't want to, and he was hardly a teenager. 'How old are you?' She said it without thinking and then winced at her own rudeness, realising he could guess at her thought process, but he gave a begrudging smile before answering.

'Thirty-three.' He even gave a half-laugh, gave her a glimpse of those beautiful white teeth, then he sighed. 'And yes, completely able to make my own decisions. It is rather more complicated though. It would seem that my party time in London is over.' He gave a shrug. 'That is how my family see it. I have, in fact, been working, extremely hard, but it's time, my parents tell me, to come back, to face duty.' He drained his glass and refilled it. 'To marry.'

'Do you love her?'

'It's not a question of love, more that we are suited. Our parents are close—it was decided long ago.' He tried to explain what he had been thinking about before she had entered the bar. 'I am happy here in London. There are many things I still wish to do with the business.'

'And you can't once you're married.'

'Once married I must assume royal duties—full-time. Produce heirs...' He saw her blink. 'I've offended—'

'Not at all,' Allegra said. 'I've just never heard it referred to as that—"producing heirs." The term's usually "have children."'

'Not when you will one day be king.'

'Oh.' She seemed to be saying that an awful lot, but really, she had no idea what else to say. It was not exactly a world she could envision.

'I am told I cannot put the official engagement off.'

'Can't you just end it?' Allegra asked. 'Just call it off?'

'For what reason?' Alex asked. 'It would shame her if I said I simply did not want to marry her. She does not deserve that.'

'Does it worry you?' How utterly he intrigued her! 'I mean, if you don't love her, are you worried about...?' She wanted him to fill in the word, but of course he did not. 'Well, I do read the magazines. I might not have known you were a prince, but I do know the name, and if I remember rightly, you do have a bit of a reputation. Does it worry you settling down?'

'Fidelity?' He was so direct, so straight to the point, that she could not help but fidget. She scratched her temple and tried to think of a better way of wording it, but settled for a nod instead, to show him that was indeed her question. 'That won't be an issue—as long as I am discreet.' She was far too expressive, because she screwed up her nose.

'You're walking into a marriage knowing you are going to be unfaithful....'

'It's a duty marriage. Anna has been chosen for she will one day make a most suitable queen. It is not about love,' he explained, but her lips were pursed. 'You don't approve?'

'No.' It had been *her* champagne, he'd chosen to join her—she had every right to be honest, every right to give her opinion if he chose to sit here. 'I don't see the point in getting married if that's how you feel.' She was speaking from the heart—Allegra actually had very firm views on this. She adored her parents, but their rather unique interpretations of marriage vows had had her crying herself to sleep so many times growing up that, on this, she would not stay silent.

'Our ways are different. I am not saying that I will…' He never discussed such things, his family never discussed such things, but there were unspoken rules and his betrothed understood them. 'I don't expect you to understand. I am just talking, not asking for a solution.'

He watched as the pout was replaced by a very reluctant smile. 'Touché,' she said, and after a brief hesitation she nodded, perhaps ready to listen without judging now.

'Our family is very much in the spotlight.'

'Believe me, that part I do understand. I know all about families and spotlights,' Allegra grumbled. And she told him—well, a little, but far more than she usually told another person. After all, if he was a prince then he had far more to lose from indiscretions than she. It actually wasn't down to half a bottle of champagne or a handful of nuts and wasabi peas; it was simply the company, sitting in their little alcove, huddled together and putting the world to rights. It was a tiny pause before they headed back out there.

'My family loves the drama. My sister Izzy was on a talent show….' He had not a clue what she meant. 'To find a pop star.'

Alex shook his head; he rarely watched television and if he did it was only to see the news. 'Why would that impact on you?'

'It's not just Izzy. My dad used to play football in the Premiere League,' she explained. 'He's like royalty here—

except…' She hesitated then looked into his eyes, saw his brief nod and knew she could go on. 'It's just one scandal after another. Last year there was an unauthorised biography published about him.' He watched the colour swoosh up her cheeks. 'It was terrible….'

'Inaccurate?'

'Yes,' she attempted then shook her head. 'No—it was pretty much all true, but you know how things can be twisted.'

'Is that why you didn't want to report your boss?'

He was way too perceptive, Allegra thought.

He was also right.

'They've had a field day with the Jacksons recently.' She told him about the scandals, about her mother, Julie, and the affair that her father had had with Lucinda, that he was now married to Chantelle, but still *friendly* with Julie. She talked about Angel, who was Chantelle's daughter, and Izzy, who belonged to both Bobby and Chantelle. Allegra even had to get out a beer mat at one point and draw a little family tree. 'The book made it all sound so grubby.' She looked down at the beer mat, saw that perhaps it was. 'It really hurt my dad—oh, he said it didn't, did his usual "any publicity is good publicity" spiel, but I know it upset him. I'm trying to put it right.'

'How?'

'I want to write an authorised one—I've started it actually. I've got loads of memories, hundreds, if not thousands, of pictures.' He saw the flare of something he recognised in her eyes—that mixture of focus and passion that met him in the mirror each morning, the commitment that meant it was killing him to walk away from his work. 'I want to set the record straight.'

'Well, you've worked in publishing so you've got the right contacts,' Alex said. 'Write it.'

She laughed, as if it were that easy. 'You've no idea how much work—'

'You don't have a job!' He smiled but she shook her head; he simply didn't get it—and why would he? It hurt too much to sit and talk about impossible dreams, so instead she asked about him.

'What about your family tree? I'm sure it's a lot less complicated than mine, a lot less scandal.'

'Actually...' He stopped then, for the most bizarre moment he had been about to tell her, about to speak about something that was completely forbidden, even within palace walls, *especially* within the palace walls—the constant rumour that his sister Sophia was possibly the result of an affair with a British architect. He looked to her green eyes staring out from beneath her heavy fringe and thought how nice it would have been to tell her, to admit as she so readily had, that his family might not be completely perfect.

'It's pretty straightforward,' he said instead.

'Lucky you.' Allegra sighed. 'I'm the boring, reliable one, of course. They won't believe that I've lost my job.' He watched her snap her eyes closed on panic. 'If I don't get a job soon I won't be able to keep up my rent and I'll end up back at Dad's and be sucked back into the vortex.' He did understand that feeling, her eyes told her that he did, for he leant over and his eyes held hers.

'That is how I feel. That is why I don't want to return just yet. I know that the moment I do...'

'I know,' Allegra said, and she spoke some more, except he was only half listening, his mind elsewhere. He looked to the table where he had sat just last week, with a man on the edge of his dreams who now lay cold in the ground, and he looked to the window and he saw the rain. He did not want to be lying there, cold with the rain and a life half lived, dreams undone. He wanted more for his business, wanted a couple more years before he returned to the fold—but how?

'Can't your brother do it?' She pulled him from his introspection and she saw him frown. 'If you don't want to be king…'

'I never said I did not want to be king,' Alex corrected. 'Just that I would like more time.' He frowned at her. 'Matteo and I have had different upbringings. Of course, were anything to happen to me, he would step in, but…' He tried to explain it, for though he never expected her to understand, today he *wanted* her to. 'You said earlier, that is how people feel at funerals…that people get upset…'

'Of course,' Allegra said. 'Everyone does.'

'No.' He shook his head. 'When I was seven my grandmother died. The funeral was massive. At the cemetery…' He did not really know why he was telling her this; he had not thought of this for years, but somehow he had to make her understand. 'Matteo was upset, my mother hushed him, then my father picked him up—I remember because it was one of the pictures in the newspaper. I started to cry,' Alex said. 'Not a lot, but a little. The coffin was going down and I could hear my brother, and…I started to cry and my father gripped my hand and then he gripped it tighter.' He took a breath. 'He was not holding my hand in comfort.'

'I'm not with you?'

'When we got back to the palace, before the guests arrived, my father took me to the study and removed his belt.' Alex wasn't saying it for sympathy; it wasn't a sob story she was being told. It was facts being delivered. 'He said he would not stop till I stopped crying.'

'You were a seven-year-old boy!' She was the one who was appalled—not Alex.

'I was a seven-year-old prince who would one day be king,' Alex explained. 'He had to teach me difficult lessons. A king does not cry, a king does not show emotion....'

'You were a child.'

'Who would one day be king,' Alessandro said again. 'And around and around the argument goes. You can despise him for it, but it was a lesson my father had to teach—which he did. He taught his firstborn son—perhaps he knew it was a tough lesson, for he gave my brother more rein at least till he was older. I have what it takes—I have been raised for this purpose.'

'I'm not surprised you want more time.' Allegra blew up her fringe. 'Before you have to go back to—'

'I could always fall in love.' His voice halted her mid-sentence. 'Our people know it is not a love match—Anna knows that too. Surely if I met someone and fell in love... there would be scandal, but it would blow over.'

Allegra looked to him. 'Maybe you should try talking to Anna.' She gestured to the table behind them, to the ladies that had been vying for time with him. 'Maybe she's the one...?'

That made him laugh.

'I will not fall in love.' He said it so assuredly. 'I have no time for such things. But if I *said* that I had...'

There was a flag rising, an alarm bell ringing, but they were slow and in the distance because by the time she registered them, she had already spoken on.

'Said that you had what?'

'Fallen madly in love. That love had swept me off my feet, that I had become engaged.' He indulged in a smile at the ridiculousness of the very thought. 'Of course, in a few short weeks I would come to my senses and realise I had made a mistake, that my new fiancée and I are not suited after all, or more likely the people would strongly object. But by then it would be over between Anna and me, and my family would want me here, in London, at least for a year or two, till things had settled down.'

'Well…' Suddenly her throat was dry. 'Good luck looking.' She watched as he went to top up her glass, except the bottle was empty and he summoned the waitress but Allegra shook her head. 'Not for me.' She needed space, because her mind was bordering on the ridiculous. For a moment there she'd thought he was talking about her, that they were plotting together, that this might be real.

She excused herself and fled to the safety of the ladies', told herself to calm down—except when she looked in the mirror her cheeks were flushed and her green eyes glittered in a way they never had before. Her fringe was stuck to her forehead from the rain and she blasted it under the hand dryer, then dabbed on some powder in an attempt to calm her complexion down.

Had he been suggesting that she…? Allegra halted herself there, because it was ridiculous to even entertain such a thought—yet… Who'd have thought when she stepped inside the bar, or when she had walked out of her job, that just a few hours later she'd be sharing a bottle of champagne with the Crown Prince of Santina.

She would have hid in the ladies' for a little while longer, would have straightened out her thoughts before heading back out there, but a couple of the women Alex had been avoiding came in then and didn't shoot her the most friendly of looks.

'I said that I didn't want any more champagne.' The waitress was about to open another bottle when she returned.

'Just leave it there unopened,' Alessandro said to the waitress as Allegra sat down. 'We might have something to celebrate later.'

'Not with me you won't,' Allegra said.

'We could just take it back to my—'

'I think you've very much got the wrong impression of me,' Allegra said primly, so primly she hoped he could not hazard a guess as to her suddenly wild thoughts, because she would love him to pick up that bottle, would love to dive into a taxi and be kissed all the way back to his place, to sit and drink champagne on a sheet rumpled by their lovemaking. God, but she'd had too much to drink and, mixed with this man, she was having trouble attempting rational thought. 'Half a bottle of champagne and I'm well over my limit—and I don't leave bars with men I've barely met.'

'I was joking,' Alex lied, for he *had* been hoping. 'What about my other suggestion? Do you want to be my fiancée?'

'Alex…' Allegra said. 'Why, when I didn't even want to have a drink with you, do you think I'd even entertain—'

'A million pounds.'

She laughed, because these things didn't happen, and he had to be joking. When he pulled out a chequebook, she laughed even more, because it was crazy. Except when he handed it to her, his hand was completely steady and he wasn't laughing.

'You might not have to do anything. I will fly to Santina tomorrow and tell my family and Anna. The people will be outraged. Soon enough I'll be told to reverse my foolish decision, to come back to London till the scandal dies down.'

'So what are you paying me for?'

'I can't just invent someone—you might have to join me in Santina at some point.' He anticipated her reaction, because as she opened her mouth he spoke over her. 'You would have your own suite—a couple cannot be together until they are married. All you would have to do is smile and hang on to my every word.'

'Until?'

'Until the people dictate otherwise.' He gave a shrug. 'It might be days, it might be weeks.' He looked to the cheque and so, too, did Allegra, and she thought about it—hell, she really thought about it. He wasn't asking for her to sleep with him, just to smile and hold his hand. And what she could do with the money… She could get a flat, a job—actually, she could do what she really wanted….

'You could finally write that book.' It was as if he had stepped into her mind. She heard his voice as if he was inside it, but it was madness, it couldn't work.

'We'll make it work,' he answered her unvoiced words. 'Is that a yes?' Alex asked.

She looked back at him, thought not just of the book she could write but a link to this man, this beautiful man who had entered her life, and somehow she simply wasn't quite ready to let go of him. 'I think so.'

They stepped out onto the street, and she was wrong about taxis, for a luxurious car was waiting and it took them just a few streets down.

'Shouldn't you deposit it?' Alex asked.

'Okay.' She grinned and walked into the bank and watched the eyebrow of the cashier rise a good inch. 'Funds won't be available till the cheque is cleared.'

'Ring my bank and get it cleared now,' Alex said, and she looked at the name on the cheque and did as told. There was the strangest feeling in her stomach as the cashier handed her a slip with her bank balance, a sort of great weight she hadn't been aware she'd been carrying suddenly lifted.

'Now, we shop.'

'Shop?'

'A fiancée needs a ring.'

They poured back into his car, laughed all the way along the street.

'Shouldn't I have royal jewels?' God, she was tipsy.

'You should, but…' They were outside a very smart jewelers. 'At least this you will be able to later sell. The acting starts here,' he warned as he pushed a bell and the door opened. She stood there and looked at rings as the jeweler came out, and the acting did start here, because he held her hand as he spoke with jeweler, told them what he had in mind and they were whisked away, to view jewels kept well away from the window.

'What about this?' Alex turned to his fiancée but he had lost her attention, her eyes drawn not to the diamond ring he was holding, but to another that to Allegra was far more exquisite.

'It's heavenly.' She picked it up—a brilliant emerald, so huge that it looked like a dress-up ring, but Alex shook his head.

'Should be a diamond…'

'Oh!' She put it back down, remembered her place, that this was not real; she was merely playing a part. He put his head to her ear in a supposed romantic murmur. 'Diamonds are more valuable.'

'Perhaps.'

And he saw her longing for the ring, saw the moss of Santina in the jewel of her eyes. Perhaps an emerald would be more fitting and he hesitated for just a moment. After all, what did it matter? Soon it would be done, she would be gone, so she might as well have a ring to her liking.

He slid it on her finger.

'We'll size it,' the jeweler said.

'No need,' Alex said. 'It fits perfectly.'

'I'll give it a polish and box it,' the jeweler said, but Alex's hands were still holding hers, and they looked for all the world like a young couple in love, on the edge of their future, and she felt this wash of emotion for all that was not.

'I don't want to take it off,' she admitted.

Allegra was confused and a little embarrassed to face him after he'd paid and they'd stepped outside.

'Well done,' Alex said. 'You almost had even me convinced, though that is not the ring a future queen would choose.'

'It's heavenly.'

'It's yours,' he said. 'Let's get you home.'

She gave his driver her address and of course they couldn't discuss it in the car, so as they pulled up to her little flat and presumably because he was her fiancé, he saw her to her door, or rather the entrance on the street.

'I'd rather you didn't come up…it's messy. I wasn't expecting—'

'I don't care!' He hushed her excuses.

He didn't care and Allegra knew that—not about the mess in the flat, nor the chaos he was creating. Nor, she must remember, did he actually care about her.

'What happens now?'

'You write your book.' Alex smiled. 'I'll fly to Santina in the next few days and break the news. I guess we should swap phone numbers.'

She tapped in his and when she had finished he picked up her hand and looked at the ring now on her finger. 'It's actually very beautiful.' He looked more closely and then still held her hand and looked at her, saw she was suddenly nervous, perhaps regretting what she had done. 'It really is just for a short while. Allegra, thank you.'

And she knew his kiss was coming. It was a kiss goodbye, a kiss to seal the deal, euphoria perhaps. It wasn't just his smile that was dangerous, his kiss was too.

He lowered his head down and his mouth was warm and firm and just so absolutely expert. She breathed in his scent and she felt his lips and knew in a second he would end it. It was just a kiss to seal the deal, Allegra told herself.

He moved his head back, their lips parting, and she watched as he pressed his together, as if tasting her again. He smiled down at her, just a little, a warning smile, for he indulged again, lowered that noble head to hers. And it was a kiss called euphoria, she told herself, for it was not really her he was kissing, but a glimpse of the freedom he craved. And she kissed him back, because he made her weak, because the stroke of his tongue was completely sublime. He put his hand in the small of her back as if to steady her—and thank goodness he did, for if the previous kiss could have been covered by a handshake, then this one moved completely out of bounds.

His tongue was cool and his hand was warm, and when one hand would not do to hold her, when more than gravity was needed to anchor them to earth, he kissed her all the way to the wall. This dance of lips and hands in hair, two locked mouths and the strength of a wall to hold them up as he kissed her more thoroughly than she'd ever even dreamt of.

Heavens but it was thorough, so thorough that for decency's sake it had to end. She looked up into eyes that were wicked, as if absolutely he knew what he'd do with her, all things she would never allow and it was imperative that she correct him.

'What I said before about us not...' She swallowed. 'I meant it. I don't want to give you the wrong impression.' With that kiss, she knew she just had. 'I think I've had too much champagne....'

'You're a strange mix.' His hand was still in her coat; he wanted to lift her jumper, slide his hand to her skin, but Alex was also sensible, very used to women falling in love with him. In a situation such as this one, that would never do. 'You are right,' he said, 'it might confuse things.'

CHAPTER THREE

'ALLEGRA!' She woke to the ringing of the phone and there was no time to gather her thoughts before answering. 'Allegra, it's me, Angel, what on earth's going on?'

'Hold on a moment,' Allegra said. 'Someone else is trying to get through.' She looked at the caller display, saw it was her brother Leo at the same time as she saw the ring on her finger and heard the bell that meant someone was at her door.

Oh, God!

'Angel…' She couldn't explain it to her stepsister right now—yes, they were close and they spoke about so many things, but this was more the sort of situation Angel might find herself in, not the other way around. 'I've got someone at the door. I'll have to call you back.'

Even as she put down the phone it was ringing again, her father this time.

She didn't answer it.

And she tried to ignore her doorbell, just wanted a moment to gather her thoughts. A coffee would be extremely welcome, except whoever it was must be leaning on the bell, because it was ringing incessantly now. Kids meeting up at the underground for school often pressed it for the sake of pressing it, so she hit the display button to see the camera shot…and saw the face of Alex, pale and unshaven. He looked less than happy.

Well, he could have his ring back, Allegra decided—it had been a stupid game that had got out of hand.

'It's open.' She pulled on a dressing gown and turned on the kettle, then went to the front door as she heard him rounding the top of the stairs.

Somehow he looked both beautiful and terrible at the same time—his olive skin seemed tinged grey, his eyes were bloodshot and he was still in yesterday's suit.

'Coffee!' She could hardly stand to look at him she was so embarrassed—so she turned and headed to her small kitchen. 'Before we say anything, I need coffee…and by the looks of things so do you.' Her blasted phone was ringing and unable to face it she turned it off and then spooned instant granules into mugs. 'You can have the ring back.'

'Oh, no, you don't.' There was something in his voice that sounded like a warning, almost as if he were angry, and she turned around. 'You can't just get out of this.' He held up a newspaper. 'I'm assuming you haven't read the papers or turned on the news.' Allegra went cold as she saw the photo. It was of her and Alex—him tenderly holding her hand and examining the ring that now seemed to burn her on her finger.

'At least—' she tried to stay calm, to think of a positive '—at least it wasn't a few moments later,' she said, 'when we kissed.'

'My kissing a woman would hardly be newsworthy,' Alex said, 'but that the Crown Prince of Santina has bought a woman a ring…'

'It was a mistake,' Allegra said. 'We'll say—' her mind raced for possibilities '—that we're friends, that I was simply showing you—'

'I have just spoken with Anna.' Alex chose not to go into detail; the conversation had been supremely difficult and one he did not want to examine just yet, let alone share. When Allegra asked after the other woman, Alex shook his head. 'Somehow I don't think she'd appreciate your concern.'

His words were like a slap, the implications of the one reckless day of her life starting to unravel.

'I have also spoken to my parents.'

'They've heard?'

'They were the ones that alerted me!' Alex said. 'We have aides who monitor the press and the news constantly.' Did she not understand he had been up all night dealing with this? 'I am waiting for the palace to ring—to see how we will respond.' She couldn't think, her head was spinning in so many directions and Alex's presence wasn't exactly calming—not just his tension, not just the impossible situation, but the sight of him in her kitchen, the memory of his kiss. That alone would have kept her thoughts occupied for days on end, but to have to deal with all this too, and now the doorbell was ringing and he followed her as she went to hit the display button.

'It's my dad.' She was actually a bit relieved to see him. 'He'll know what to do, how to handle—'

'I thought you hated scandal,' Alex interrupted.

'We'll just say—'

'I don't think you understand.' Again he interrupted her and there was no trace of the man she had met yesterday; instead she faced not the man but the might of Crown Prince Alessandro Santina. 'There is no question that you don't go through with this.'

'You can't force me.' She gave a nervous laugh. 'We both know that yesterday was a mistake.' She could hear the doorbell ringing. She went to press the intercom but his hand halted her, caught her by the wrist. She shot him the same look she had yesterday, the one that should warn him away, except this morning it did not work.

'You agreed to this, Allegra, the money is sitting in your account.' He looked down at the paper. 'Of course, we could tell the truth…' He gave a dismissive shrug. 'I'm sure they have photos of later.'

'It was just a kiss….'

'An expensive kiss,' Alex said. 'I wonder what the papers would make of it if they found out I bought your services yesterday.'

'You wouldn't.' She could see it now, could see the horrific headlines—she, Allegra, in the spotlight, but for shameful reasons.

'Oh, Allegra,' he said softly but without endearment. 'Absolutely I would. It's far too late to change your mind.' He drew in a long breath, and even if he wasn't prepared to share it, Anna's tearful words seemed to replay in his head. "I guess you can't argue with love." He had been right; it was the only dignified way out for them both, and to have Allegra back out now, to think of shaming Anna even further by releasing a story that implied he had bought his way out of marrying her, was unthinkable.

She could hear her father running up the stairs; he ran everywhere, was fitter than most men half his age. 'What the hell's going on, Allegra…?' Bobby's voice petered out as he realised his daughter had company. She wanted to run over to him, to tell him, to let him sort it out, except it was Alex who walked towards him.

'Mr. Jackson, I apologise that you had to find out this way.'

'It's true then?' She watched a look that could only be described as incredulous sweep over her father's face, could see him actually try to fathom that his serious, rather plain daughter had just got engaged to a prince. Somehow his shock hurt Allegra, that it might be so impossible that she might actually be desired by someone as stunning as Alex.

She felt Alex join her, his arm slip around her waist and when she couldn't speak he did. 'We were going to come and visit you this afternoon,' Alex explained. 'I was going to formally ask for your daughter's hand.' Allegra saw her father's eyes widen, saw Bobby rather taken aback by Alex's formality, but he was saved from responding as Alex's phone rang and he excused himself to take the call.

'Gawd!' Bobby pulled a face. 'He's not your usual—'

'No,' Allegra said. 'In fact, he's not remotely interested in football.' There was a distinct edge to her voice, because all too often she had found that her dates were rather more interested in impressing her father than her. 'Look—' she swallowed '—we were hoping to take things a little more slowly. It's all got a bit out of hand....'

'That's what happens when the press get hold of things.'

'I know it's a shock, Dad,' Allegra said. 'I'm sorry—'

'Sorry!' Bobby laughed. 'Why on earth would you be sorry? He's a bit straight-laced, but...' His voice trailed off as Alex came back to the room.

'I've spoken with the palace, Mr. Jackson.' He took her hand as he addressed her father. 'Given the news is already out, they think we should formally announce it. There will be an engagement party just as soon as it can be arranged.'

'A party...' Allegra felt his hand tighten around hers. *No!* she wanted to shout, and not just to halt things here. Alex had no idea what he was suggesting, no idea what her family could be like.

'A party!' Bobby's face lit up, and Allegra found she was gripping Alex's hand back. She wanted to pause things, to get not just the cat but a hundred kittens back into the bag, because Alex needed to know what he had let loose.

'I can't imagine...' Her voice was a croak and she turned

urgent eyes to Alex. 'Perhaps something smaller, we don't need to do anything grand.'

'Nonsense.' It was Bobby who answered. 'Why wouldn't you want to celebrate, Allegra? I've got loads of contacts, we can find somewhere—'

'In Santina,' Alex interrupted, and she watched her father's jaw tighten just a fraction. 'Of course, we would love to have your blessing...for your family to join us in Santina to celebrate our engagement.'

CHAPTER FOUR

'YOUR family behaved appallingly.'

Alex hissed it out of the side of his mouth as they headed back to their suites.

'Which is exactly what you wanted,' Allegra said. 'Which is exactly why you made sure there was a photographer to capture every disastrous moment. Well, I hope you're pleased.'

'Oh, I can think of many other words to describe how I'm feeling.' Alex was, in fact, conflicted—he had, to his guilty shame, hoped for a little scandal, just to prove to his family and the people of Santina how completely mismatched they were. He couldn't believe how well his parents had taken the news. His mother had burst into tears on his arrival, thrilled that her son had returned home, and his father, though never effusive, had taken him aside and told Alex he was privately relieved that his son was ready to assume more royal duties. He did not admit as such, but reading between the lines Alex wondered as to his father's health. Not for the first time since Alex had arrived in Santina, realisation was dawning that it *was* time to return and fulfill the role he was born to. But it would now be without the polished presence of Anna—a woman who understood the role, understood the people of Santina's ways.

Instead, tomorrow the papers would be filled with the Jacksons' shenanigans, for they had delivered scandal in spades, and of course it would reflect on him. His family must have thought he had gone insane. Matteo had been appalled; his best friend Hassan had outright asked him if he had completely lost his mind.

'They weren't that bad,' she attempted. Yes, her family had been shocking, but they had also been so happy for her, so genuinely delighted, unlike the royal guests, and Alex's friends—who had all sneered and frostily responded to the Jacksons' exuberance.

Guests were still milling around, spilling out from the ballroom and heading, not just for the manicured gardens but, given it was Allegra's family, no doubt to fill the palace's cornered-off rooms. Despite defending them Allegra was mortified by her family's behaviour—from the arrival of the Jacksons on the island, to their loud carry-on at the very formal party, it had exceeded her fears. Now, as the happy couple walked out, as they headed to their separate suites, as the charade neared its conclusion, suddenly Allegra felt like crying. 'Yours were no better.'

Alex actually stopped midstride and turned around. 'What on earth is that supposed to mean? My family were gracious.'

'They did nothing but look down on mine.' She struggled to keep her emotions contained, a hallway, no matter how lavish, was not the best place for this discussion and there was the photographer from *Scandal* magazine still milling around. But right now she didn't care who heard. 'Matteo hauled Izzy away from the microphone, dragged her away from her own sister's party. All she wanted to do was sing….'

'It's a royal engagement, not a drunken karaoke night! We'll talk about this later,' he said, struggling hard not to shout. But really the palace had never seen anything like it! 'For now, just…' He looked down to her strained face and decided against asking her to resume the besotted facade as she looked positively close to exploding. He simply didn't get it—after all, it was her family that had disgraced themselves. From her drunken sister taking the microphone and attempting to sing, to her father's rambling attempt at a speech. Thank goodness he wasn't actually marrying into them. 'Let's get upstairs….'

She didn't want to go upstairs, didn't want to again be banished to her turret, to the room she'd been pacing since she'd arrived in Santina. She'd hardly seen Alex, or Alessandro as she had been told to call him now. This was practically the first time they'd been alone together and knowing her family was about to be so publicly ridiculed, that tomorrow they would be torn apart in the newspapers and magazines, she was way past acting for the cameras.

'I've never met such a frosty, uptight lot.' Allegra would not be silenced by his stare, would not accept his derisive words, even if they were merited, and it brought the sting of angry, defensive tears to her eyes. 'At least my father wished us well.'

'He was drunk,' Alex pointed out. 'He said—and forgive me if I misquote—but if I remember rightly, he was thrilled that you'd done so well for yourself.'

'At least he tried,' Allegra said.

'Tried?' Alex could not believe what he was hearing. 'He couldn't even make it back to his hotel—he's sleeping it off in a guest room! I've got a driver going over there to pack a night bag for him. And you think he tried?'

'That's my dad,' Allegra attempted, for how could she even begin to explain to this cold, arrogant man the irreverence that made her father so appealing—at least, it did back home. 'At least he didn't just peer down his

nose and…' She couldn't finish; if she did she'd make a
fool of herself and start crying. The whole night had been
wretched. Her whole time on Santina had been wretched—
almost the second they had landed he'd turned into one
of them. What had happened to the man she had met in
London?

'You've changed.' She said it accusingly but it just
served to irritate him.

'Of course I have—here I am Crown Prince…'

Didn't she know it!

He was as cold and aloof as his father. Even tonight as
she'd been presented to the king, shy, nervous—petrified,
in fact—he'd barely passed comment on her transforma-
tion. Dressed in a lavish deep red gown, her hair smoothed
and gleaming, still she clearly hadn't passed. She'd seen the
slight sniff from his father, the disapproving looks from
his family, and she could have put up with that, with just
a few words of encouragement from Alex. If it had been
real, if they had been in love, it would have been unbear-
able to be made to feel so second rate.

If they had been in love.

'Well—' she caught up as he marched off '—you got
what you wanted.'

He wanted the conversation left there; he had something
rather difficult to tell Allegra, a rather unexpected turn of
events that she wasn't going to take too well and he certainly didn't want to say it here, didn't want to be seen in
a corridor rowing—they were, after all, supposed to be
in love. But her words confused him, demanded closer
inspection, and maybe some of Bobby's inhibitions had
rubbed off on him, maybe one night with the Jackson clan
and he was starting to act like them, for he momentarily
forget his station, forgot that he must always be one step
removed from any conversation. Even though he had taken

her wrist and started walking, Alessandro found himself stopping again.

'What do you mean by that?'

'You planned it.'

He would not row here, so instead he opened a door, any door, and went to drag her in, but he was greeted by the sight of a couple—well, the arms and legs of a couple—and they were too far gone to even notice they'd been invaded.

'Good God!' He closed the door and stood in the corridor; the palace had been turned into a seedy nightclub. As he turned, expecting to see her look of horror, he was less than amused when she rolled her eyes and gave a wry grin.

'You think that's funny?'

'At least they're enjoying themselves.'

'Doesn't it abhor you?'

'I think it's lovely.' She didn't actually, Allegra just wanted to shock him now, wanted at least some reaction. 'At least they know how to have a good time.'

He refused to be drawn. Instead, as the corridor was empty, he asked for clarification to the statement that had incensed him. 'What do you mean I planned it?' He could not believe what he was hearing. 'I'm making sure the events manager is fired in the morning! No one would plan for this!'

'You made sure there were photographers…' Allegra pointed out.

'To show that we're madly in love.' Sarcastic though his response he stopped himself, actually gave a brief shake of his head, for he was not going to be drawn.

'It was your plan to shame my family…to make sure that tomorrow there'd be no question that I wasn't suitable.'

'Your family took care of that all by themselves,' Alex said, but that knot of guilt tightened. 'Come on.' He took her hand to lead her, but she was not about to be dismissed.

At the end of the hall they would turn off, would separate, him to his royal suite, she to her guest room, and there was just too much to be said to leave things here.

'I want to talk.'

'We will talk.'

'I don't want to leave things till tomorrow.'

'We won't,' Alex said, and then, because he had no choice but to tell her, he did. 'Now that we're officially engaged we'll be sleeping together.'

'We bloody well won't!'

'Not sleeping together...' he said hurriedly, and at least managed to look a little shamefaced. 'I had an argument with my parents. I was trying to point out how archaic things are, how ridiculous it is...' He watched her face, watched her eyes widen, her mouth open to speak; he could feel her tension, like a can of fizzy drink being shaken and shaken and any moment now she would explode, just fizz out her anger all over the corridor. 'I was talking more about the chosen-bride thing,' he tried to placate her. 'This is my parents' attempt to show me they've moved into the twenty-first century. Now that we're officially engaged we can share a bed.'

'No...' Her reaction was instant, there was absolutely no question, but as she spoke he heard a noise behind him, turned and saw the *Scandal* photographer about to come into the corridor, just as Allegra exploded. 'If you even think for one moment that I'm going to share—'

He had no choice—there was but one way to silence her. He pressed his mouth to hers, but she was having none of it, and jerked her head away, her protest about to continue. So he pinned her to the wall, took her face in his hands and just pressed her right in.

And pushing him off with her rigid lips wasn't work-ing. Alex was tall and strong, so she opened her mouth instead to shout, except he kissed her harder; his hands moved faster than hers and captured her wrists as they moved. He wedged her to the wall and she was furious. Yes, he'd paid her, but not for this!

She did not care if there was a photographer—she'd give them a shot! She wasn't Bobby Jackson's daughter for nothing; she could be as rough as she liked, and her knee went to move upwards, ready to take aim.

There was only one thing that saved him—he ceased the kiss before contact, his reflexes like lightning, and he froze her with a single word. 'Don't.'

She looked at him and for the first time since landing on this bastard of an island he actually looked back.

'Don't you dare,' he muttered.

'Well, that got a reaction,' she taunted. 'Worried about the crown jewels?' she goaded, speaking now into his ear. 'I'm surprised they're not protected.' She was aware of the cameras flashing, and somehow she did behave, didn't finish the job off and storm away from him. Instead, because she could, she stood there, because he dared not move. 'Or perhaps they are…' She gave a low laugh, her hand moving as if to check him and he gripped harder on her wrist to stop her. Not just because the camera was trained on them, not just because a Crown Prince could not be seen being groped in the corridor, but because he was rock hard.

He looked to green eyes that were spitting; he looked and he looked again. He heard his own fast breathing, and now he could feel hers, feel her breasts pressing into his chest with each rapid breath, and he was not thinking, he was just up for the challenge. He dropped her wrist because he wanted her hand instead, except she wasn't so brave now, her hand not moving to its target.

'I thought I was going to get a pat down.'

'There's a camera.'

'It doesn't take photos around corners... They can't see that side.'

'You're disgusting,' she said.

'I can be.'

He said no more, not that Allegra would have heard him anyway; her head was spinning, her ears roaring as blood gushed to her head, her face on fire as a butler opened the door to a private wing. She passed several rooms, and then double wooden doors were opened and she stepped into his bedroom. Had she had a moment to ponder, she would have realised it was perhaps the most beautiful room she had ever seen. The ceilings were high and there was intricate wooden paneling and a fragrant fire was lit to ward off the chill of the late-spring evening. The drapes and furnishings were exquisite, but she barely glanced at them. It was the vast bed that terrified her most and she was also acutely, painfully aware of the palace maids waiting. She had hoped the door would close, that she could have angry, private words with Alex, because this was so not a part of the deal, but instead she was led to a dressing room—her dressing room, it would seem—for Alex headed to another.

She stood, horribly awkward as the zipper of her dress was slid down.

'I can manage now, thank you.' She did not need someone to undress her, except the maid didn't leave. Instead, as Allegra slid out of the ball gown, the maid retrieved it and then handed her a small nightdress that certainly was not one Allegra had brought.

'I can manage now, thank you,' she said again.

'Of course,' the maid responded. 'I need the jewels.'

'Sorry?'

'For safekeeping.'

Left alone, her dress and jewels removed, she could hear

Alex undressing, telling his servant his choice of outfit for the luncheon tomorrow, clearly used to stripping off and dropping his clothes at whim, only to have someone pick up for him.

She took off her underwear and slipped on the night-dress, both nervous and furious at the thought of sharing a bed with him. She wanted her own space to curl up into bed and go over the night by herself. And yes, she wanted to recall their kiss, to relive the feel of his lips, the dizzying absolute pleasure of it even if it had just been for the camera. She wanted to recall it alone, needed a little bit of space before she could look him in the eye again, but instead she had to spend the night with him. She could hear him closer now, thanking the valet, telling them he would not be needing them at all tonight.

'Just breakfast at seven,' came his snobbish orders. 'Oh, and the newspapers, of course.'

She heard the door close and then silence, but Allegra stood there.

'Allegra?'

Still she stood there.

'It's just us now.'

Which was why she was nervous to go out there!

He did not need to know of her nerves; instead she'd show him her anger. She walked out of the dressing room, feeling completely awkward in a short lacy nightdress. Why, she hadn't worn a nightdress since she was about four years old, and certainly not one that came midthigh with tiny straps that would surely snap if she dared roll over in the night. She was rather more used to T-shirts or pyjamas for bed.

She was also more accustomed to bed and a book alone than this vast one that had Alex sitting up in it, reading through texts on his phone. Naked, at least from the waist up, he glanced up as she walked in and then went back to reading his texts. 'And I thought communal changing rooms were bad. She expected me to undress in front of her. Don't you know how to take your own clothes off? They took my dress and jewels....' Alex didn't answer. Since their time here he hadn't indulged in small talk and she'd had enough. 'This,' Allegra said in a voice that was more than a little shaky, 'was not—'

'I know that,' he cut in. 'But there's nothing we can do about it now. Don't worry,' he said. 'I'll sleep on the sofa.' Well, he would in a moment, but right now, the sight of her in that skimpy nightdress, the beauty of her as she had stepped out of the dressing room, meant that, for a couple of moments at least, the decent thing to do was stay under cover and read a garbled text from his brother as she nervously chatted on.

Allegra sat on the edge of the bed, indignant still at the maid's implication. 'As if I'm going to flee in the middle of the night with the Santina royal jewels.'

'I wouldn't put it past your father...' He gave a small laugh. 'Or Chantelle. She used to have a market stall, you said. Maybe...?' He had meant it as a joke, something to lighten the tense mood, but glancing up he saw her face screw up, and his apology was immediate. 'I'm sorry, Allegra, that was—'

'A joke—' she looked at him '—that's all my family are to you.'

'No.'

'Yes.' She closed her eyes for a second. 'That speech of Dad's...' How could she explain her father, how inappropriate he was at times, but how lovable and kind he was too? 'He's a nice person, if any your cold-fish family gave him the chance.'

'Cold!' Alex raised his eyebrows, even bristled a little,

perhaps learning that it was fine for him to insult them, but it touched a nerve when others did. 'My mother cried her eyes out when I returned—that's hardly cold.'

She wasn't going to argue about his family, and it was a waste of time and energy to sit here and defend hers.

'Your bedroom is stunning.' She looked around, because it was far, far safer than looking at him, so now she did take in the extravagance of her surroundings, the gorgeous fire crackling in the huge ornate fireplace, and her eyes drifted up to the carved ceilings and huge lights.

'It's not mine—well, clearly it now is.' She jerked her eyes to him, to where he sat on the bed, his chest gleaming, his shoulders wide and strong and chose to look away. 'It's my first night in here—I've inherited it apparently. This is actually the royal wing.' He looked to where she frowned. 'This is where the crowned ruler sleeps—though they've handed it over a little early.'

'This is your parents' room?'

He gave a mirthless laugh. 'Quarter of a century ago. Once they'd had their children they moved to separate wings. This one has been cornered off since then. They used to use it though—my mother didn't want central heating when it was installed, said that it was bad for the complexion, which is why we're bloody freezing.'

'Your parents sleep apart?'

'I shouldn't have mentioned it.'

'For when I go to the press?'

'I don't for a moment think that you shall, but if you could avoid telling your family…'

'How effortlessly you insult them,' Allegra said.

'That wasn't my intention. You're right, my family aren't exactly warm. They get on with the serious job of ruling Santina. There isn't time to be worrying about—'

'Oh, come on, Alessandro…' she was even starting to

use his real name '…surely you make time, surely when those gorgeous wooden doors close…' She didn't continue; there really was no point, for were she queen, were Alessandro her king, no matter how hard the day, no matter the weight of responsibility… It was pointless considering it, pointless because tomorrow morning the press would baying for her to leave.

'They have better things to worry about than keeping the romance alive.' He rolled his eyes at the very thought and turned his thoughts to the morning when the people's verdict would come in—undoubtedly demanding he renounce his right to the throne if he insisted on taking such an unsuitable bride.

And she was most unsuitable, Alessandro reminded himself.

He had paid her to be her unsuitable self after all.

Even in the finest gown, she had looked all wrong in the heavy red dress. He had rather preferred her in those shapeless tweed trousers she had had on when they'd met—not corseted and quaffed, all her curves hidden and held in. But now she sat on his bed, her heavy fringe to one side, her dark curls a little wild now they had been let down, and without all the jewels at her throat, without the confines of the dress, her body was so alluring, so feminine beneath that skimpy gown. She was slender, yet soft; he could see dimples on her thigh that, were this a true romance, the paparazzi would later persecute her for. Her breasts through the skimpy nightdress were larger than he'd imagined. And yes, more than once in these past weeks, to his own annoyance, he'd imagined them—just not to this delicious detail, for her nipples seemed constrained beneath the lace, as if attempting a breakout. Just as it had seemed safe to climb out of the bed, it became terribly unsafe again.

'I thought you were going on the sofa.' She was sick of

this, she was tired too—and the bed was huge, about the size of five of her own, so she peeled back the sheet and climbed in. 'I guess we can just treat it like a school camp. You don't get to choose who you share with.' She looked over to him. 'I suppose you didn't go on school camp.'

He didn't answer, having returned to his texts, and it was Allegra who pulled out her phone and plugged in an earpiece.

'What are you doing?'

'Well, conversation isn't exactly forthcoming, so I might as well go to sleep. I like to listen to music to fall asleep,' Allegra said, because as tired as she was, there wasn't a hope of her falling asleep unaided with Alex in the room. 'Well, not music exactly—' she was a little nervous, for still he was in the bed '—more the sounds of nature.' He gave her an extremely quizzical look, so she elaborated. 'I listen to the sound of the ocean, it relaxes me.' She gave a little laugh. 'At least till the recording stops.'

'You could just open the window,' Alex said. 'Ah, but you're a Londoner.' Because things had calmed down somewhat he climbed out of bed, and even if he was feeling a touch more appropriate, suddenly Allegra wasn't. His black silk pyjama bottoms rested on his hips and accentuated the length of his legs, and though he had looked beautiful tonight, he was beyond that now, his back gleaming, muscles teasing as he walked across the room and flung open the French windows. She was terribly grateful for the blast of cool air that swept the room, for her face was burning—grateful, too, for the roar of the ocean, for it must surely drown out the sound of her heart that was hammering in her chest.

'The real thing is always better,' Alex said.

The real thing was standing before her now, the absolute dream, the man, the life she could only briefly glimpse, but how she wanted it to be real, for she could still taste his kiss, still and forever would remember the bliss of being held by him. And now he stood, utterly relaxed, maybe even a little bored, as she tried to steady herself on the vast bed. All tonight had done was accentuate how utterly different they were, the gulf between their backgrounds, how impossible this match was—and it would be proven tomorrow, had perhaps been proven already, for, as Alex had pointed out, many of *her* guests had been snapping away on their phones. No doubt the scandalous Jacksons were a trending topic on Twitter! They lived in two different worlds, but for tonight at least they met in this room.

He collected a throw rug and tossed a few cushions to one side of the sofa. When his temporary bed was made, he gave her forewarning.

'I've set my alarm for six-forty,' Alex said. 'They come in at seven, so don't get the fright of your life when I climb in. We don't want to disappoint the maids.' He tried to make a joke of it, but how the hell was she supposed to sleep with this glorious specimen of a man in the room? A man who had kissed her, a man her mind wanted to dream of…? How was she supposed to rest knowing that in— she glanced at the clock—just over four hours he would be climbing in beside her? ''Night then.' She leant over to the night light, her finger on the switch as Alex was about to lie back on the sofa.

'Goodnight, Allegra.'

She was leaning over to turn off the light and just as she had silently predicted, but earlier than even her imagination had allowed for, the delicate strap on her nightdress snapped, one heavy breast escaping. Mortified, she did not look up—hoped, just hoped, he wasn't watching. Somehow she turned off the light, mumbled a goodnight and dived under the sheets, listening to the waves, to the soothing relentless ocean, desperately trying not to think of the man in the room.

The man in the room who could not sleep either.

His last image before being plunged into darkness was of a very soft breast, just sort of dropping, just falling, and he had wanted to hurtle over to the bed, like some American baseball game, hurtle across the space and capture it in his hand.

How the hell was he supposed to sleep after that?

CHAPTER FIVE

'YOUR Highness...' The butler was appalled, stunned, that as he served the queen her early-morning tea on her alfresco terrace, just as he did each morning, a jogger was making his way through the queen's private gardens.

'I'll call security now, come inside....'

'It's fine.' The queen was not perturbed; instead she was vaguely amused by the break to her routine, and somewhat confused when she realised who it was jogging their way across the manicured lawn. Shouldn't he be in bed nursing the most appalling hangover?

'It's Mr. Jackson,' Zoe explained to her anxious butler. 'He mustn't have realised that this area is private.'

'I'll tell him now.' The butler went to do that, went to raise his arm to the man, but the queen always remembered her manners and if she recalled rightly, because he had been in no fit state to make it to the hotel, Bobby had become a last-minute guest of the palace and would be treated as such.

'Mr. Jackson,' she called, except he didn't seem to hear her. 'Bobby...' How strange that name felt on her lips, but she called it and he turned and gave her a very cheery wave and she gave a rather more tentative one back, a little taken aback when he jogged his way over.

'Morning, Zoe!' He'd called her Zoe, and he must have

realised his mistake, for quickly he moved to correct it. 'Oh, sorry, I mean…'

'Zoe's fine—' she smiled '—at least when it's just us, but when there are others around…'

'I'll remember that.' He gave her a very nice smile; in fact, she wasn't quite sure, but did Bobby Jackson just wink? Suddenly the queen was acutely aware that she was dressed in her nightdress, albeit with a heavy silk dressing gown on top. Still, he was wearing very little too—shorts and a vest, really—but the queen had far too many manners to even blink.

'Would you like to join me for some tea?'

Bobby didn't hesitate; after all, he was incredibly thirsty! 'I'd love to.'

He glanced over her shoulder, perhaps expecting the king to appear. 'Out walking, is he?'

'I'm not sure,' she answered, and Zoe, unusually, found herself flushing a little—a touch embarrassed that it was perhaps obvious she slept alone. Bobby frowned and then she was suddenly terribly aware of her attire, because the frown and the look he gave her were more akin to disbelief than pity, more a look that Zoe was terribly, terribly unused to. Oh, there was nothing improper—well, not really; his frown seemed to say he had no idea why the king would leave her alone, and it brought a fire to her cheeks and a slight shake to her hand as she sipped her tea while the butler brought over another cup.

'Did you enjoy last night?' Zoe enquired.

'I can't remember it yet,' Bobby answered, and he started to laugh. After a brief moment Zoe found herself laughing too, though it faded when he continued. 'I don't think my speech went down too well. I didn't even get to finish….'

'We're not really used to impromptu speeches.'

'You wait till you come to ours,' Bobby said, and then he glanced up. 'I'm sorry—' he blew out a breath '—it's a bit awkward, isn't it? I mean, you try to get on with the in-laws, but...' He grinned at the thought of Her Majesty in his mock-Tudor home. 'We'll work it out.'

'I'm sure we shall,' the queen said, though privately she doubted the wedding would even happen. She had seen the stars in Allegra's eyes, but whether it was parental instinct or just years living a life void of emotion, something told her that there was more to this engagement than even Bobby knew—maybe Allegra even—for her son was not one to be guided by his heart. There was more going on and she knew it. Still, sipping tea that morning was bizarrely the high point of the party for Zoe—Bobby Jackson was perceptive and funny and really quite charming, and at times surprisingly pensive too.

'Allegra gets on with her stepmother?' The queen had approached the complicated subject of Allegra's rather extended family.

'She does.'

'And you still get on with your first wife?' Zoe's voice was just a little strained; perhaps she was being impolite asking, but it just intrigued her so, that a man could bring his current wife and his ex-wife to a party, and from the way Bobby behaved with Julie, well, she was quite sure they were still lovers.

'Julie's golden.'

'I see.' Zoe frowned. 'And the other boy...' She blushed because she was fishing, but she'd seen him with Anna, and it was such bliss to gossip. It had been so very long since she had. 'Leonard?'

'You mean Leo,' Bobby corrected. 'The one making eyes at your son's ex?'

The queen hardly recognised the sound of her own

laughter. 'A man that takes notice! So...' She had long ago waved away the butler and it was Zoe that poured more tea. 'Leo's from your first marriage?'

'Er, no...' She heard his cup rattle as he replaced it in the saucer. 'His mother's name was Lucinda—she was a lover of mine.'

'Oh.'

'She's passed away,' Bobby explained. 'Leo's been with me ever since. It took me a while to come to terms with it—I mean, I said that he wasn't mine. She never disputed it, so I assumed I was right. It turns out that she did a DNA test. I should have been there for Leo....'

'Aren't you cross that Lucinda never told you?'

'I admired her for it,' Bobby said, and he looked to the queen. 'There's something about a woman who can keep her silence, something rare about such a woman.' And he was a touch awkward then, remembering suddenly the rumors he had read when finding out a little more about Allegra's fiancé. But the memory actually helped, for he wasn't awkward any more. He looked at the queen and thought there might be a teeny flash of tears in her eyes, and he looked again, for she really was a very beautiful woman. But there was such a sadness to her and, queen or not, Bobby knew how to talk to women. 'I regret a lot of things, but I can't regret how my son was raised—she did a wonderful job. I've made my share of mistakes, but I guess we all do.'

'You can't when you're a queen.'

'You're a woman first.'

'Oh, no.' She shook her head, but Bobby didn't leave it.

'Well, you look like a woman to me. Whole lot of trouble, all of you!' He saw her pale smile. 'Anyway, guilt causes more problems and solves none of them. I need to be a parent to him, not try to be his friend. Like I said, we all make mistakes—'

'We do. Indeed,' Zoe broke in, and they shared a small smile.

'Not Allegra though,' Bobby said. 'If that's what's worrying you. From when she was a little girl I used to say to Julie, that girl was born to be a mum! You should see her with her brothers and sisters. She doesn't seek the limelight, our Allegra, doesn't go looking for drama. She's a great girl, more sensible than the lot of us put together—your son's going to be a very happy man. Anyway...' Bobby stood. 'It's been a pleasure to get to know you a little better, Zoe. I'm looking forward to spending more time with you and your family.'

He was rough, he was crass, but he was completely and utterly charming, and Zoe could see why his women forgave him. Absolutely she could see why his country adored him.

She'd never hinted, not to a soul, that she was anything less than perfect, that mistakes might even be made, yet somehow this morning...

She felt liberated.

She liked the Jacksons' energy that was in the palace.

She liked Allegra too.

She looked at the papers and picked up her tea, her hand shaking a little as she read of the people's reaction to the union, the in-depth pieces, the endless photos and the headlines that screamed, and wondered how the young couple would deal with this morning's news.

The queen often meddled, at least where her children were concerned, and leaving her quarters she crossed the palace, heading to the kitchen, meeting a maid at the lifts.

'You know we have several extra guests this morning.' She gave a reason as to why she was there. 'Where are these going?'

'For Prince Alessandro,' the more senior maid informed her. There were two of them to take up the huge trolley, laden with coffees and pastries and the newspapers; the butler would of course take it in. 'He asked for breakfast at seven.'

'Leave Prince Alessandro.'

'He asked to be woken at seven.' The maid was nervous, but used to this, for often the queen interfered.

'Give him an hour.' The queen smiled, because if she was right, then just about now, Alessandro would be crawling into bed—and if she was wrong, oh, well! 'They did not get to bed till late. If there are any repercussions, just say it was on my orders.'

She watched as the maids wheeled the trolley back towards the kitchen and went back to her quarters and sat down, picked up her set of the newspapers and carried on reading.

Alessandro and Allegra surely needed that hour together, before they had to face this.

Allegra did sleep, not much, certainly not enough to prepare for the wretched day ahead and the barrage of press and demands from his family, but she did sleep a little, listening to the ocean, seeing the shadows of the fire dance across the room. Then she heard a few bleeps of his alarm and then nothing, for Alex did not seem to awaken. She wondered if she should tell him, remind him perhaps, for any minute the servant would be in, but she lay there in silence instead, holding her breath when finally he moved. He closed the windows, for the room was freezing, and stared at the bed where she lay on her side.

He was stiff and cold, a throw rug not really up to a

draughty palace in spring, and neither his long frame nor his status were used to roughing it on a sofa.

Still it was not that which had him irritated, more a night spent trying not to picture her breast, and that body, and when he did close his eyes…

He padded across the room in the dawn light, pulled back the sheet and climbed in. The bed was cold and he lay there a moment. He heard her stir a little, knew that she was awake, and he said what had been on his mind all night. 'I'm sorry, Allegra.'

'It's just for a few minutes.'

'I meant for everything. I know how hard these weeks have been. I know it's not a life that you're used to.'

'It would have helped to have seen you a bit more,' Allegra said, 'and I'm not being needy. But—'

'I know you're not. It's the way it is here—I've had a lot of duties to attend to, as well as trying to keep up with things at work.'

'I can't even go out without an escort. What do they think's going to happen?'

'The people might recognise…' He started with the familiar line, the one his father had drummed into him all these years, except he was older now, could see things more clearly. 'The royals used to be more accessible, there was more freedom, but it does not work.'

She turned over to face him. There was a guardedness in his voice and she wanted to know more, to understand better, but he said no more; it was clearly a closed subject.

'I couldn't live like this.'

Alex was silent.

'I couldn't.'

'Most women would be—'

'I'm not most women,' Allegra said.

'No,' he admitted, 'you're not.'

She turned back from him then, wished she hadn't seen his face on the pillow beside her, for it danced now in front of her closed eyes, a vision she would always remember. Because though she could never live like this, there was a part of her that wanted it to be real, that wanted Prince Alessandro who lay beside her to be her real fiancé, a woman who wanted the dream…

…who wanted him.

He looked at the clock and saw it was almost seven and it would look strange, surely, for two newly engaged people to be sleeping so far apart on the bed.

'Sorry about this.' He moved over, not sorry at all; his feet were freezing and he heard her breath catch as they slipped in between her calves. Her side of the bed was so warm, and for appearances' sake, for his own sake, but not for decency's sake, he moved his body in.

He was male, used to waking next to a woman, not used, though, to a night spent frustrated and alone—so many nights recently, in fact. It was hell being back at the palace—especially as a newly engaged man—and the feel of her next to him, the scent of Allegra and the warmth of a woman, well, it was good. 'You're warm.' He wrapped his arm around her.

'You're freezing.' His foot moved against her calf and she didn't halt him. His long arm slid between hers, his hand looking for a place to settle and she did not move away when it found a home just a whisper away from her breast.

'Did you get some work done?' He had, to his credit, always asked about how her book was going. 'Did you ask your brother about his mother, Lucinda?'

'I didn't really get a chance to talk to him. You should do your family history.'

'It is all documented already.'

'The real version though,' Allegra whispered. 'There are surely things only you know, things only your sisters or brother know. Your parents—'

'Just leave it, Allegra.' She hadn't been prying, she'd just been talking, but feeling him tense, Allegra realised she had stepped on a raw nerve. It was none of her business, of course; she was paid to be his fiancée after all. But more and more she wanted to know him, wanted to understand the workings of this remote family, wanted more of his life. Except there was no more talking and she wondered if he had gone to sleep.

There was something about morning, something special about lying there, waiting for the maids, something a little sad, because here, this very morning, it all came to an end.

Today, she would hear in detail just how very unsuitable she was, which was the plan, of course. It just hurt, more than she had expected it to—and she knew she had to hold on to her heart here. But for a moment, at least, it was nice to pretend that it was real, that Crown Prince Alessandro really did love her, that her family's behavior didn't matter to him a jot—that the man lying beside her, whose ring she wore on her finger, did not deem her such an unsuitable bride. It was a dangerous flight of fancy, and as his hand moved to her breast, as his palm caressed what he had been thinking about for hours, she really ought to push him away, except it was nice to suspend, nice to feel something, safe in the knowledge they were acting, that really it could go nowhere. For any minute now the doors would open, any minute now they would be sitting up, sipping coffee, reading papers, and then the maid would be back to dress her.

She tried to the think of the morning ahead, of the rows that would ensue, of the plane flight home and that soon she would be away from the palace, free from the lie, ready to resume her life, except his palm was on her breast, and his thumb was stroking her nipple and it was nicer to just live in the now. His cold feet moved a little, just a little higher and made her catch her breath again, for they really were cold, and he was idly stroking her naked breast with his hand. No doubt it was just sheer habit, no doubt he was already back to sleep, and just idly fondling whatever was available to him this morning,

But goodness, it felt nice.

'Alex.' She moved his hand away; it was relaxed and he did not answer her.

Asleep she decided, suddenly cross, because what was so effortless and natural and inconsequential to him was having the most dizzying effect on her; even the weight of his hand on her stomach, the weight of him so close, had her wishing she had not interrupted him.

And in sleep he must have felt the same, for his hand wandered back to her breast and his body awoke behind her, and he moved just a little more in.

He was not asleep, but more rested now than he had been all night.

He was loving this side to Allegra, the warmth of her body in the bed, the surprising softness of it, for yes, she was slender, but there was a ripe softness to her and a very unspoiled scent, just a natural fragrance he was unused to.

'Alex.' Again her hand went to move his, except instead it captured his. She did not want an accidental encounter; she had more pride than that at least. 'Someone will be in soon.'

'They'll knock.' She knew then that he was awake, but it was easy for him, so natural for him. Just for a moment she let herself glimpse it, that this was their bed, that the lips near her ear, that the hand on her breast, were just where they should be, that this moment was theirs.

'Wouldn't they expect us to be kissing?' Alex asked, for her kisses had always surprised him, kisses that seemed to unbend her, and now, this morning, his body craved her mouth.

Though she lay so still, her mind wrestled, for she wanted him so, wanted his kiss, wanted a little of what she could never really have.

'Perhaps!'

He turned her to face him. His mouth did not claim hers; instead for a moment they just stared and it was as if they were saying farewell. Allegra felt a sting behind her eyes.

'I make a terrible fiancée.'

'You'd be a wonderful fiancée,' Alessandro said. 'If I wasn't a royal.' He brushed her fringe out of her eyes and he kissed her forehead, easily the most tender thing he had done to date. But more than that, he kissed it again, and then he kissed her eyes, kissed the salty damp lashes and tried to explain, without rowing, just how impossible it was. 'Having you here has been like a breath of air.'

'I've hardly seen you,' Allegra said.

'Which is how it would be…' He looked over to her on his pillow. 'You've been wonderful.' He settled for this instead and she knew that this really was goodbye. His mouth moved to where her lips were waiting, and he kissed them thoroughly, one ear on the door. But then the door was forgotten because of how lovely and warm and how deep was this kiss, how nice the feel of his leg wrapping around hers and hooking her in; he kissed her till her body was more awake than it ever had been, kissed her till their lips were so wet and her fingers knotted in the back of his head.

'Someone…' she reminded again, and his head lowered as he took to his mouth the nipple he had dreamt of all night. It tasted as sweet as he had imagined and for Allegra it felt sublime, especially as he moved his mouth away and then blew, and then kissed and teased her nipple again, as he caressed it with lips that were soft now and tender. He took it deep in his mouth again, and she could feel the scratch of his unshaved chin on her tender flesh.

'Someone might….' she attempted.

'But they would knock,' Alex reasoned, and he tasted her some more. His hands moved around her waist and then played with her bottom, lifted up the nightdress, slid it over her hips, and his fingers pressed into bare flesh. He heard her breath in her throat and he sucked harder; he felt her so warm and aroused in his arms and he willed the door not to open for just a few more precious moments, especially as her hands roamed his torso, as he felt wary fingers slowly work their way down.

She knew they would be interrupted, actually hoped it might be Alex who would remind her of that, that he would halt her hands and stop this nonsense. Instead he moaned as her hand slid into black silk pyjamas and freed him.

Please knock, she thought as he left her breast, as he slid her up the bed and faced her in the darkness while she still held him in her hands. She did not know what to do now, so she felt instead, ran her fingers down the delicious length of him, stroked, so gently, from the tip to the silken hairs at the base and back again.

The bed was not moving, really they were doing nothing, Allegra told herself. If the door opened now, they could release and just close their eyes, pretend to be asleep.

'I think we've been forgotten,' Alessandro said, for once delighted by inefficiency. 'They must be busy this morning….' He ran a hand along his fiancée's thigh and kissed her on the mouth. He succumbed to her tentative exploration, only just hearing a noise in the corridor outside. Allegra heard it too, for she released him, rolled over onto her side and closed her eyes, ready to pretend to be asleep, except her heart was hammering, her body in full arousal.

She was more than a little shocked at the turn of events, almost willing the door to open, so she could get on with her paid duty, not succumb to the bliss of him. For how nearly she had, Allegra thought, screwing her eyes closed tighter, surprised by her own inhibitions. They waited, waited for the door to open, except there were no further noises, no one outside now, and in silence they lay still.

'We can't,' she said as a warm hand slid around her waist. 'They'll be here any moment.'

'I know,' Alessandro said, but he did move in just a little closer, his erection nudging between her legs, his hand snaking to the front of her, down her stomach to a place that was warm. His exploration was not as tentative as Allegra's; he moved slowly but deliberately down, and long fingers so easily found the magic button that had her pushing herself backwards just a little to him, had her parting her legs. When his mouth kissed her shoulder he slipped his erection deeper between her thighs, nudged his way like a homing device to her entrance, and she felt her throat tighten.

Alex never lost his head, ever.

Except, as he lay in the bed, in the bed of a king, with Allegra beside him, for a little while he did lose his head. Centuries of history, perhaps, created a loud whisper that drowned out common sense, for he smelt the pine from last night's fire and the creak of the wood that lined the walls. He felt the nightdress bunched around her waist move against his stomach, her bottom pressed to him. She was so damp beneath his fingers, he wouldn't last a moment once inside; Alex acknowledged that rare fact, for normally he could go for ages. But there wasn't a hope this morning, so he gave her more urgent attention instead, his fingers

more insistent, and when she came, when he brought her
to that place, he would enter and join her.

'We can't…' Her words were contrary, for her body was
on fire in his hands.

'They'll knock.' He didn't care if the whole of Santina
walked in on them. In that moment he did not care. He
could feel the tremble in her, the tension in the thighs
that clamped on his erection and on fingers that were still
working. He was as close as she was and he wanted to be
inside her. He guided himself to her entrance, moved his
face over hers and felt the heat from her cheeks as she
spun her head around to him and he suckled her tongue
in hungry possession.

She could feel the press of him, the nudge of him, and
she wanted him inside her, wanted to scream. She had
to tell him to stop, except she was gasping as his fingers
brought her close now to heaven, and she felt him press at
her entrance. She really had to tell him, her voice breathless when it came, her hips arching away from his hand
that was pressing her back to him.

'Alex, no…'

He was aware of three things.

In one second, there were three things.

The word *no*, when she was so wet and oiled there surely
should only be a plea; the knock on his door that told him
their privacy was about to be invaded; anger, too, for the
games she was playing, for the kisses that ended, for the
glimpse, for the taste…

…for the tease.

CHAPTER SIX

'I ASKED for breakfast at seven.' He sat up in the bed and lifted one knee to hide the obvious as Allegra lay there, eyes closed, wishing she *was* asleep, wishing as clearly as Alex did that the breakfast *had* been on time, that the last hour had not happened. She heard the harshness of his tone, and knew it had nothing to do with the late breakfast.

'I apologise, Prince Alessandro. The queen said—'

'The queen stopped dictating the time I eat my meals many years ago,' Alex snapped.

'Of course, Your Highness.' His butler bowed. 'Will there be anything else?'

'Nothing,' he snapped. 'I am not to be disturbed.'

He hardly waited for the door to be closed, too used to servants, too ready for confrontation, to attempt patience.

'Talk about lousy timing, Allegra.'

'I assume we're not talking about the door?' He wasn't in the mood for even a vague stab of humour. 'Look…'

'Have you any idea how…?' He was having great trouble keeping from shouting. 'It's a bit late sometimes to change your mind.'

'I know that.'

'Some men…'

'I know!' Her voice was shrill, her cheeks on fire. She simply couldn't tell him her truth, that he'd been about to find out she was a virgin, that there had been no *other men*, that though she had wanted him terribly, she had been scared it might hurt. She put her face in her hands for a moment; she understood he was cross, for she was cross with herself too. She was the last person to lead a man on; it was just with Alex it was so very easy to lead and to follow and then to lead some more, to lead and be led until completely lost, to return hungry kisses, to listen to her body and not her mind. No, she couldn't land all that on him, couldn't tell him he was the only man she'd burnt for, the man who would live for ever now in her dreams. Instead she offered a more sensible reason, which was obvious now—except it hadn't been then. In fact, the thought hadn't entered her head at the time, but she said it now as if it had.

'We weren't using protection.'

He closed his eyes for a brief moment and drew in a deep breath.

'It would complicate things rather, a little Prince Alessandro, Junior…' Allegra warmed to her rapidly chosen subject.

'You're not on the pill?'

'No, I'm not on the bloody pill. I'm not seeing anyone, and I'm certainly not going on it just in case…' She looked over to him. 'Have you heard the one about the prince who walks into a bar…?'

'Ha, ha!' He did not approve of her London humour.

'Anyway—' Allegra smarted, far safer up on her high horse '—it's not just for pregnancy.'

'I don't need a lecture on safe sex,' he hissed.

'Actually, Alex, I'd suggest that you do.' How lovely it was up here, she thought, how lovely to have been so embarrassed, but to now be peering down from a higher moral ground. But it was as if he reached out and jerked her down from there, brought her right back to his bed with a flash of his eyes; she could see the concern in them, felt a little guilty that the rapid excuse she had come up with should provoke such a response.

'I apologise...' He swore under his breath in Italian, and raked a hand through his hair. He moved to the side and sat on the edge of the bed, his head in his hands. 'I always, without exception, have been careful. You have nothing to worry about there.'

'It's fine.' She wanted to reach out and touch his shoulder, could see lines where her nails must have dug in, could scarcely believe the wanton woman he had made her, but the touch to his shoulder was a kinder one. 'Alex...'

He turned his head and she saw that he was beautiful—he was a man who could have not just her body but also her heart in an instant, and she could not let him take all the blame.

She felt his skin beneath her fingers and there was arousal still hovering in the room like a rare mist awaiting its beckon to descend. If she pressed her fingers down just the merest fraction harder, she could blink and it would be summoned. 'I don't know how much of me I can give,' she admitted. 'Just to have it handed back...'

He paused before he gave her a nod that said he understood.

'We have to be affectionate in company...' Her voice faltered. 'We have to pretend we're in love, we have to share a bed...and any minute now, when your family have decided I'm too much trouble, or when the people dictate, I'm going to be sent back. There's only so much I can give in the meantime.'

She stretched over him and selected a paper, leant back on her pillows as he did the same. She braced herself for the usual scandal when the Jacksons hit the headlines—

except she sat speechless as she read the headline, holding her breath, worried to turn her head and see his reaction as he selected a newspaper of his own.

Bravo, Allegra!

Alex put the paper down and took another.

Will the People's Princess Give the Prodigal Prince a Reason to Stay?

And the headlines were shocking, utterly and completely shocking—just not in the way he had predicted.

'What does *Bella Sposa* mean?' Allegra asked.

'Beautiful Bride.' He cleared his throat as he skim-read the articles. 'This one says that the people of Santina await the wedding with deep joy. They love you. I can see that. They think you are the answer to the monarchy's problems, the breath of fresh air the people want....' He swallowed. 'I did not even know that the people were so unhappy.'

He read on: 'Apparently a wedding is what Santina needs....' He was visibly appalled at the prospect. He balled the paper in his fist, scrunching it up, and she felt as if he were squeezing her heart, for his reaction told how her appalled he was at the very idea.

'Us!' He looked at Allegra, a woman who talked about *feelings* and what life could be like behind closed palace doors, a woman who straight up had told him she believed in fidelity, a woman who had said, only moments ago, that she could not live like this. She had no idea how it would be! If she thought this was impossible, then how could she even begin to deal with the road ahead if she were groomed to one day be queen?

He cursed again, stood and paced the room—for he had not just put Allegra in an impossible situation, he had failed the people of Santina too. Not necessarily today, but in the future. He glimpsed it then, the palace ricocheting from one scandal to another, from one headline to another, and he could not put them through this.

'This was not how it was supposed to be—can you imagine?'

She found her voice, right there beneath the shame his reaction had triggered, right there behind the sting of tears in her eyes, and she hauled it to the surface.

'No!' She sounded as if she meant it. Hell, she meant it as he flung the paper across the room. 'We agreed to a few days, a couple of weeks—it's already been far longer than that.'

'I will sort it.' Alex wasn't waiting for the butler; he was pulling on clothes and dressing in haste. 'Right now, right this very morning, I will sort out this mess.'

She jumped at the slam of the door and then stared at the papers that were scattered across the bed, looked at the pictures of them. One especially drew her attention: the happy couple arriving in the huge ballroom, Alex looking down at her. She remembered his words of reassurance, the small squeeze to her waist, and something she must have said in response had produced his rare smile—the same smile that had enthralled her the day they had met. And clearly, it had enthralled her last night, her rapt expression was there for all to see, her eyes sparkling as brightly as the huge chandelier that glittered above them. In that moment Allegro knew the real reason she was here, why she had agreed to the charade, why she had found it impossible to walk away.

Why she climbed out of bed to get dressed herself, for now that the initial shock was wearing off, now that the people's verdict was sinking in, she wanted to speak with Alex before he spoke with the king.

She wanted to speak with her fiancé.

* * *

The king considered it a done deal.

'We need to set a wedding date.' He was pacing, distracted, when Alex came into his study. 'I want you to speak with Antonio, to go through our schedules....'

'We're nowhere near ready to be speaking of dates,' Alex said. 'Allegra needs time to get used to things, to really see if this is the life for her.'

'It became her life when you put that ring on her finger,' the king said. 'It became her life when you ended things with Anna. It's not open for discussion any more. I've got enough on my mind without pandering to your fiancée—Prince Rodriguez is arriving tomorrow to meet Sophia.'

'So?'

'Your sister has disappeared and now I cannot get through to Matteo either.' He looked to his son. 'Last I saw him was with that Jackson girl, the one who was singing—'

'Izzy,' Alessandro said.

'The palace is in a shambles. We need to give the press something to distract them. As soon as they hear the wedding date, that is all they will talk about.'

'I am not giving a date just to appease—'

'You are engaged!' The king swung around. 'Under the circumstances you should be grateful the news has been so well received by the people. Now, I think sooner is better.'

'There will be no announcement till I have discussed things with Allegra.'

'Why would you need to discuss things with her?'

Alex gritted his teeth. 'Because it is the twenty-first century.' He gave a grim smile as his mother joined them.

'The people are delighted.' She greeted him warmly. 'You must be thrilled.'

'Allegra's feeling a bit overwhelmed,' Alex attempted. 'I think last night gave her a glimpse into how it might be and she's not sure that's she's suited.'

'Then ensure that she is,' the king snapped. 'Can she lose that accent?' he said. 'Preferably by lunchtime.'

'It's not just her accent,' Alex said. 'You've seen her family. Her father—'

'I had tea with Mr. Jackson this morning.' The queen smiled. 'He's actually rather charming.'

Alex was tired of flogging the 'it's clear she's totally unsuitable for this life' angle. 'It's not just Allegra feeling it—it was a mistake. Last night has shown me that. I'm taking her back to London.'

'Running away again! Shirking your responsibilities!' The king was not about to let this happen.

'Hardly. I run a multibillion—'

'Don't try to impress me with figures. They do not come close to Santina's worth. This is your duty, and you will not shirk it a moment longer.' He was harsh, but he knew his son was needed, knew what a wonderful ruler he would make. And there was an element of truth in the papers—the royal family wasn't as beloved as it had been. The king knew that and he wanted his son to step in and help, but he could never admit that. 'It's too late to change your mind. You wanted the engagement, you chose this path. Now you either make a date for the wedding and live here in Santina with your bride or you leave and go back to London.'

'Fine.' It was actually far easier than Alessandro had thought. They would leave this afternoon; he'd stay in London till things had calmed down. Alex turned, ready to head back to Allegra, to tell her the news—except his father hadn't quite finished yet. He wanted Alessandro here.

'I am not subjecting the people of Santina to two broken engagements from their heir.'

'Meaning?'

'We had two sons for a reason.' Alex glanced to his

mother, saw the humiliation scald her cheeks, for that was how his father spoke at times. He might love his daughters but bitter had been his disappointment that they had not been sons. 'If you end things with your fiancée, I insist you step aside.'

'I will never step aside!' He had certainly not anticipated this outcome. In that bar, with Allegra, he had been certain, absolutely certain, that his father would demand that they part, that if they insisted on going ahead with the marriage, then he would have to step down. He had promised this to Allegra and now he had been outmaneuvered, and he had to go back up there and tell her. But first he would try to dissuade his father. 'How can I marry her?'

'You should have thought of that when you asked her!'

'It was different in London,' Alex said. 'I see now that here she doesn't fit in. I don't love her....'

'Thank goodness for that,' the king said. 'You can keep your mind on the job then.'

'Alessandro,' his mother urgently interrupted, but Alex was not listening.

'Look, I've realised my mistake—she's completely unsuitable.'

'Well, it's too late for that,' the king said. 'The people—'

'You really want that vulgar family to be welcomed into ours? You really think Allegra would make a suitable queen?'

'Alessandro!' his mother said again, but Alex's mind was only on one thing—he had no intention of stepping aside.

'I am supposed to spend the rest of my life with this woman, a woman so ordinary?'

He heard a gasp.

He knew it was her, before he even turned around.

'Allegra...'

'Please don't…' She put her hand up to stop him. 'I think enough has already been said.'

She didn't run from the study; instead she walked in a daze back to the royal wing, and looked at the bed that was crumpled and scattered with newspapers. To think that she had lain there and held on to a glimmer of hope, that she had actually been going to tell Alex not to say anything too hasty!

He'd have laughed in her face had she told him she would consider it.

'Allegra.'

He didn't knock; it was his bedroom after all, his palace, his people….

Her heart.

'What are you doing?'

'What does it look like?' She was flinging her clothes onto the bed. 'I need a suitcase, my passport…'

'You're not going anywhere.'

'Oh, yes, I am.' She'd tried ringing Izzy, Angel, her brother Ben, but no one was picking up, so instead she would sort it herself. 'I'm going to go over to the hotel—'

'Excuse me?'

'I'm going to tell my family.' Absolutely she was. 'My vulgar family.' She was trying not to cry.

'What you heard down there…I was trying to make my father see how hopeless it was. What I said about you and your family—'

'Was said with such conviction,' she finished for him. 'I'm going to speak to them now. I'm going to tell my dad what I should have told him in the first place.'

'Really?' Alex cut in. 'Perhaps tell him he should ring his friend too, give him forewarning.'

'His friend?'

'The one who wrote the unauthorised biography—he's going to be busy over the coming months....'

'Don't try to threaten me.'

'I'm not threatening you, Allegra. I'm telling you how it will be—because if you think this is all just going to disappear when you tell your father the truth...' He paused for a moment to let his words sink in, to let her glimpse how it would be—and it *would* be! 'My father will not allow the people of Santina to be subjected to two broken engagements in the space of a few short weeks. I agree with him. There are things going on right now, repercussions from last night, that need to be dealt with.'

'What repercussions?'

'Don't concern yourself with that now, we have enough to deal with and the best way to do that is to set a wedding date.'

'No, no.' It was more a moan than a shout, horror sinking in. 'You can't expect me to go along with this now, after hearing what you just said. The next thing you know I'll be marrying you just so we don't upset the people.'

'Would that really be such hell?' It was as if she'd been delivered a terminal sentence instead of the chance to one day be queen. Still, rather than overwhelm her with that, he attempted logic. 'Allegra, I accept that their reaction is unexpected—however, people are fickle. They change their minds easily. For now they are happy, today they celebrate. What you do not understand is that one false move, one indiscreet comment, one mistake, and their minds will change like that.' He snapped his fingers in her face. 'Then, it will be a different conversation I'm having with my father. When my father realises just how unsuited we are, there will be no other alternative than to wait it out here, or to end things and return to London.'

'But that's what you want?' Hope finally sparked. 'Surely.'

'If I break our engagement, I will have to step aside and Matteo will be next in line—but that is not going to happen.' He stood and watched as her mind raced through the labyrinth and sought escape, but he blocked every exit. 'I was born to be king, and I will not give it up, no matter what my father says. But now that I am back in Santina I will assume my full duty as Crown Prince. As my fiancée, you will ensure that there will be no repeat of last night, there will be no more embarrassments, no hushed arguments in palace corridors. You will do me proud.'

'Then how—?' She floundered. 'If I'm busy being perfect, how can we expect the people to change their minds, especially if this is the only way you will still get to be king as well as break off our engagement?'

'They will.' He said it with certainty, such certainty, but it did not appease.

She forced her way through an awkward formal lunch, tried to be polite and focus on conversations, but she was too bewildered by the turn of events to pay much attention to the fact that a fair proportion of both her own and Alex's family were missing. If anything she was relieved, for if she saw Angel now it would be impossible not to break down and confess it all.

Her father gave her a warm hug at the end of a very long day. 'I'm so proud of you, Allegra.' He shook the king's hand and for an appalling moment it looked like he might kiss the queen, but Bobby gave her a brief smile instead and thanked her for her hospitality and then looked over to Alex. 'Look after her, or you'll have me to answer to.' It was affectionately said, but not well received.

'Of course I will look after her.' It was rare guilt that

tightened Alex's throat, for unlike Bobby, he knew this father really was kissing his daughter goodbye, was handing her over to him, to his family, to the people. Of course Bobby would see her again, just never like this. For as Allegra insisted on walking out to the limos with them— her high heels noisy on the marble floor, her voice just a little too loud, her stance a touch too familiar as she thanked a servant—Alex almost missed her already, missed the woman who had walked into that bar and forced his attention, missed the woman he had held this morning in bed, before everything had changed.

Somehow he had to explain things to her, but the subject was closed for now. He saw the shimmer of tears in her eyes as the limos departed and then she pleaded a headache and went to bed. The lights were off and her back was turned when Alex came in.

'Allegra?' He was not going to sleep on the sofa and he knew she was awake, for no one lay so rigid in a bed if they were asleep. 'I know you're awake.

'For now we need to set a date,' he continued. It really was not open for discussion and it burnt in her stomach so much that she started to cry. 'I will stall it for as long as possible—my father was talking a couple of months. I will try for Christmas.'

'And hope in the meantime the people change their mind about me—and then you can appease them by dumping me. Oh, darling, you do say the nicest things.' Despite her sarcastic tone, it hurt that he didn't deny it. 'I didn't sign up for this.'

Alex didn't know what to say. He realised that pointing out that he had paid her a million pounds to take part in this charade would not help matters right now. 'You need to be more affectionate. There were comments after lunch today—we are supposed to be madly in love after all.'

He moved towards her, attempted to comfort her the only way he knew how, in the language he best spoke where women were concerned. His arm moved around her body, drawing her to him. He did not fully understand her tears—yes it would be different and yes it must be a shock, but in his world, he was a prize, the one every woman wanted.

'Allegra, even if it is not how you intended, surely it is better this way. You have everything you could possibly want.' He thought of her old life: losing her job, the tiny bedsit, the demands of her family. Here she had no financial concerns and would be shielded from her family's dramas—the palace would see to that. He could feel her skin warm beneath the lace of her nightie.

And she was wrong—Alex had no intention of waiting for the people to change their minds. He had spent today thinking, weighing up the problems and as always coming to rapid solutions. Soon, she would be a more suitable bride. Elocution and grooming lessons would start with haste, and there was another very unexpected advantage to having Allegra as his fiancée: he had never been attracted to Anna—she felt more like a cousin or a sister than his betrothed—but with Allegra... He pulled her a little more towards him, buried his face in her hair and found the subtle tang of citrus. Yes, there was much solace to be had, for their attraction was undoubtedly wild. He thought of her as she had been this morning, of how very close he had been to finding release with her. Soon he would be back there—except, of course, more prepared this time. She really was delicious, and it would be so easy to lose his head.

'Allegra.' She heard the slight plea in his voice and then the feel of his lips on her shoulder, felt his hand snake a little further around. She frowned as he kissed her shoulder deeper. 'Tomorrow you must see the palace doctor.' What a modern prince he was, Alex thought as he broached the subject. 'We must get you on the pill.' She turned to him so rapidly he was almost on top of her.

'Huh?' *Audacity* was such a pale word for him, because he had it in spades. She could feel his erection against her thigh, and then the crush of his mouth before she could speak, before her mind could catch up with what he had just implied.

Her mouth gaped open and he took advantage. She tasted him, fresh on her tongue, his hand moving unbidden to her thighs; she could feel his urgency, and only this morning it would have consumed her. But so much had changed since then. She moved her face to the side. 'Don't you dare!'

'I don't want to play your games.'

'Oh, this is no game, Alex.' She wriggled out from underneath him. 'There's absolutely no need for me to go on the pill. Do you really think that I'd sleep with you after today?' She was stunned.

'Allegra, for God's sake—we're going to be sharing a bed. To say that nothing is going to happen is bordering on preposterous. You know how we are when we kiss, you know how we are....'

'How we *were*,' Allegra answered, 'before you called me ordinary.' It stung, it burned, just as much to say it as it had to hear it. 'For now your family wants me as your bride and you want me to go along with it. They also want me to be more groomed and polished.' She waited till he nodded. 'Well, they can dictate many things about my life, and I've been left with no choice but to comply, given our arrangement. But they will not dictate my sex life! There, at least, I make the rules.'

CHAPTER SEVEN

THERE were many reasons he had enjoyed London, but a significant one had been that Alex did not like to sleep alone. Here in Santina he had been betrothed to Anna, which meant his visits home had been rare and brief.

But now it was worse. He did not sleep alone, but instead shared a bed with a woman he found incredibly attractive, and who turned her back each night. Yet most nights they found themselves entangled; only in sleep did her body reach for him.

It had this morning.

As the sun had risen so, too, had Alex, Allegra's body coiling into him, her breath on his chest. It had taken every ounce of his willpower to detach her, rather than face the alternative of her recoiling in horror as rather too often she did.

It was unsustainable, Alex decided later as he headed poolside for coffee and to speak as requested with the queen, only to find Allegra doing her laps.

It was completely unsustainable that he should go weeks—no, months—without reward.

He was a man after all.

More than that, he was a prince.

Allegra stroked through the water as she did each morning.

The king and queen generally did not surface till later,

and his various siblings were either away or getting on with their duties. This was the best part of her day, gliding through the water, sometimes swimming faster when another wave of anger struck.

She'd remembered her sunblock. She'd been told to wear it even at 8:00 a.m.—her skin should be pale for the wedding. Every part of her had been analyzed and criticised: her laugh was too loud, her fringe too severe, her walk too heavy. Allegra stroked the water faster, touched the side and did a tumble turn, anger surging her away from the pool wall as she recalled the humiliation of her first language lesson.

She'd thought it was to learn Santinan, the stunning dialect that sounded like Italian with a streak of French. She spoke no Italian but had learnt French at school and was surprised that she understood more than she had expected to, was looking forward to the lesson even. Except it had been her own language that was to be improved upon. The shame still burned.

And there was Alex, as cool as anything, in a dark suit.

The sting of chlorine was a relief because as she climbed out of the pool she had a reason to rub her eyes on the towel.

And Alex watched.

He'd watched his fiancée break the silent morning with her splashing. She wasn't a graceful swimmer, he thought as he glanced up from his paper. There was no elegance as she slid through the water, just far too much noise and the occasional splash that landed at his feet—especially as she turned.

'*Buongiorno...*' He'd greeted his mother and now, having watched her swim, the butler poured more coffee as his mother came over and Allegra climbed out. 'Why did you want to meet?'

'Allegra needs to sort out her wedding dress,' the queen said.

'And you need to tell me that by the pool?'

'It is where Allegra is each morning.' The queen shrugged. 'I thought I would catch you both—you have much work to do and Allegra is busy with her book.

'Allegra!' She smiled over. 'Come and join us for some juice.'

'No, thank you,' Allegra called, looking around for her robe. She was sure she had brought it down. Instead she dried off with a towel while Alex did his best not to watch.

She was nothing like any woman he was used to—most, if they did venture poolside, would be in a bikini and stretched out on a lounger. Instead Allegra looked as if she were wearing a swimming suit from her school years—it was navy blue and should have been unflattering, except it had ridden up at the back. Which should not merit a blink—on the beaches of Santina women walked around in nothing more than a thong. Except, with Allegra, it was almost a forbidden glimpse. There was a prudishness there that enthralled, and he was envious of her fingers as they pulled the Lycra down, for he would have loved his own to oblige in their place.

'Do join us, Allegra!' The queen was insistent. 'The chef has prepared the most delicious juice.' What choice did Allegra have but to go over, especially as the butler was already pouring her a glass? 'It's watermelon, with mint and just a hint of ginger.' The queen awaited her verdict as Allegra took a sip. 'Nice?'

'Yum!' Allegra agreed, and took a longer drink, for it tasted divine, especially after such a long swim. 'God, that's good,' she said, because it really was, but she saw Alex flick his paper and bury his head in it. No doubt she had chosen the wrong word, or perhaps she should be less exuberant in her praise.

She couldn't win, Allegra decided.

'I am going to work.' He stood, dressed in a suit when all he was doing was going to his study, but he spent half the day video conferencing with that blasted Belinda and his executives and clients. She grudgingly admitted to herself that he probably ought to wear a suit, but it irritated her at times.

'So soon?' The queen frowned. 'I wanted to discuss designers for the dress....'

'You know me well enough to know that wedding details do not interest me in the least. Discuss it with Allegra.'

In fact, Alex was not irritated. But he did have other things on his mind. He could see her nipples straining against the fabric of her swimsuit, could see the beads of water on her arm. Of course his mother would have no idea that the sight of his scantily dressed fiancée was proving bothersome. After all, they slept together each night, at least in the eyes of everyone else. He felt like a teenager this morning, could not look her in the eye, could not look at her at all.

He really needed to get to London.

'Have a great day.' Allegra stood. She had been told to be more affectionate but she found it so awkward at times. She dutifully went over and walked with him as far as the French doors where she would say goodbye and then return to the queen. She smiled up to him but he didn't return it and then she remembered the queen was watching so she stood on tiptoe and kissed him on the lips. Again he didn't return it and instead he grabbed her wrist.

'Enough.'

She was damp and her hair had dripped on his suit so he brushed it down with his free hand.

'Sorry to get *water* on your suit.' Allegra huffed. 'I thought I was supposed to be more affectionate.'

'Allegra. I couldn't care less about the water…but there are more appropriate times to be affectionate, and you hardly dressed and dripping wet and tasting of watermelon…' He halted his words, dropped her wrist. 'There are limits.'

Then he strode off and Allegra couldn't help but smile.

The queen smiled too, and walked over to Allegra. 'I might go and have a little rest—it is terribly warm already.'

'I thought you wanted to discuss designers…' Allegra started, then remembered her place. 'Of course, I mean, I hope you have a nice rest.'

She headed up to her suite, and surprisingly Alex was there, but he ignored her when she walked in. Instead he carried on speaking to his phone while Allegra showered and changed into a robe. She would decide what to wear later, heartily sick of the clothes that had been chosen for her, all so formal, so co-ordinated, so thought out.

She wandered into the bedroom where Alex was concluding his call and the butler had brought in her morning tea and also a glass that contained crystals fizzing in water for Alex. It was the only noise in the room when the butler left.

'What's that?'

He did not answer, just downed the drink and then spoke. 'I will be going to London in the next few days.'

'London!' Her eyes lit up. 'I'll come—'

'I am there for business.'

'I won't get in the way. I can see my family, spend some time—'

'You will not be coming,' Alex said. 'I am going for a very discreet business trip. I am trying to arrange a meeting with a sheikh who is considering buying my business—if we both go it will turn into a media circus.' He shook his head. 'You carry on with the wedding plans, writing your book….'

She was so angry. London was her home and he was the one who got to go. Instead of drinking tea and the slivers of fruit that had been delicately arranged, she headed for the wardrobe.

'Have your tea.'

'I don't want tea.' Allegra looked at the lavish array of clothes. 'I want coffee and cake,' she said. 'I want a vanilla latte and I want to choose my own cake from the display.'

'What are you talking about?'

'I'm going out.'

'The fiancée of the heir to the throne does not just "go out."' He was at his most derisive. 'You are not in your bedsit now, you don't just pop down the road to buy some milk and stop off at a cheap café on the way. This is how it is. If you need some fresh air you can walk in the grounds.' He remembered the last time she'd been this angry, when he had pressed her to the wall after the engagement party just to silence her. But that was no longer an option, so instead he headed for the door. 'I'm going to my office.'

CHAPTER EIGHT

WHEN he had gone, she tried ringing Izzy, but got her voice mail, tried Angel too, but the result was the same. She was so worried about Angel. She'd seen her talking to some distant cousin of Alex's at the party, and in true Angel style, she had married him, just like that!

Except far from hearing of her wedded bliss, Allegra kept getting long emails about how Angel was going out of her mind stuck in the countryside in the middle of nowhere. She knew how she felt—she *completely* knew how Angel felt. But unlike her stepsister, who had begged her to keep what she wrote to herself, Allegra had been told in no uncertain terms that she could confide in no one. It wasn't fear of repercussions that kept her silent; it was the burden it would place on any family member if she told them how it really was. In the end she took her tea out onto the balcony and rang her father.

'They're an odd bloody lot,' Bobby said as the conversation turned to the party and the dramas that had played out since then. 'You know that Ben is still on Santina, and he's managed to get Alessandro's sister Natalia to work for him!'

'No!' How could she not know? 'Why doesn't anyone tell me anything?'

'I guess they figure you're busy,' Bobby answered, and

was silent for a moment before going on. 'He's a cold fish that fella of yours.'

Allegra smiled because she'd used the same term. 'Only around his family,' Allegra said, which was almost true, because when Alex was nice… She looked at her ring, remembered the kiss that had come with it and the conversation before.

'Zoe's nice though.'

'*Zoe?*' Allegra frowned. 'You mean the queen? You can't call her Zoe.'

'She said I could,' Bobby said. 'We had a cuppa together. I got lost when I went jogging the morning after your party.' Allegra couldn't help but giggle; it was the first laugh she'd had in ages. 'She was taking tea out on her little balcony,' Bobby said. 'Alone…' It was then that Allegra's eyes opened and she put down the cup she was holding. She had a sudden vision of her future, for already it was happening. 'It's criminal if you ask me,' Bobby said. 'A good-looking woman like that…'

'What do you mean?'

'Well, there was no king in sight. Just her in her little silk nightdress.'

'Dad!' Allegra gave a loud whisper, had an appalling vision of the butler listening in. 'You can't say that.'

'What! I can't talk to my own daughter?'

'You weren't flirting with her….' She was still whispering. 'Dad, tell me you did not flirt.' Oh, God! Alessandro was right, her family *were* shocking.

'I didn't do anything,' Bobby said. 'We had a cup of tea and a little chat—she's a lovely lady.'

'You mustn't speak about this with anyone,' Allegra said. 'Dad…'

'I'm not speaking to *anyone*—I'm talking to you! Anyway, I've got to get on. I've got an interview to go to.'

'An interview?'

'I'll tell you about it when I know more.'

She hated not knowing what was going on, was positive things were being kept from her. She was just so sick of the confines that as the maid returned, so, too, did Allegra's fire.

'Could you have a car arranged?' Allegra asked, and when the maid just blinked, she upped her order. 'In fifteen minutes.'

'A driver?' the maid asked, and Allegra knew better than to completely break with tradition, at least within the palace walls. 'Yes, a driver—I'd like to see a little of the island. Thank you.'

Of course her phone rang a few minutes later with an aide wanting to clarify a few things.

'I don't want a bodyguard. I just want a driver and a discreet car so I can look around Santina.' Which saw her half an hour later sitting behind blacked-out windows in an unmarked royal car, streaking along the beach and up through the winding villages, through the town. She wanted to open the window, to smell the herbs and garlic, to hear the chatter of the Santina people.

'Here will do.' She opened the door at a small set of traffic lights, gave the driver a beaming smile. 'I'll make my own way back.' She ducked out of the car and walked briskly into a shop, straight through it and out the other side, finding herself in a marketplace. She started walking again, picking up her pace, checking over her shoulder and hoping she hadn't gotten the poor driver into too much trouble. Heaven! The air tasted so sweet, and the simple bliss of walking into a café was incredible.

But her anonymity lasted all of about twenty seconds, the owner blinking and double taking as she walked in.

'Benvenuto!' He welcomed her so warmly, told her to

take a seat, but Allegra wanted to see the cake selection for herself and it was bliss to stand and choose. The owner was marvelous; he was thrilled to have such an esteemed guest and did not want crowds ruining it, so he hastily closed his shop, allowing only the present patrons to remain.

She chose the house specialty, a kind of cannoli filled with pecan ice cream and dusted with icing sugar, and had the best vanilla latte she had ever tasted. She sat alone and read a magazine and it was wonderful. Wonderful to hear the chatter around her once people had gotten over the initial shock of her being there.

'Mi dispiace.' A mother dashed over to stop her daughter, who had taken the flowers out of the vase on their table and was now offering them to Allegra. 'I am sorry,' the woman said, 'of course you want privacy.'

'They're lovely…' Allegra took the bunch. *'Grazia.'* She spoke her first public word in Italian.

'We will leave you to enjoy your space,' the woman spoke in faltering English, 'but we are so happy to see you here, to have you amongst us.'

'I'm happy to be here too.'

Allegra really was—those fifty-eight minutes of freedom were the absolute sweetest she had known in weeks, though Allegra knew it could not last. She could only imagine the chaos she must have caused back at the palace when the driver informed them what she had done, so she was actually expecting the huge black car that slid beside her as she walked along the cobbled streets, bags in hand. She even managed a smile as the window opened and a boot-faced Alex issued extremely clear orders.

'Get in.'

'Pardon?' Allegra said sweetly.

'Don't make a scene, Allegra.' He had a smile plastered on his face as he pulled over and parked, and when she did not get in, just carried on walking, he opened the door and stepped out, taking her in his arms. She got a very brief taste of the mouth that she had craved, but it was cold and hard and his voice was stern as he spoke in her ear. 'Get in the car this minute. I'll speak to you when we are back at the palace.'

'I don't want to go back to the palace.' He looked down at her, chin set in defiance, eyes glittering with rage, her anger barely contained, and was reminded of the night of their engagement—the little spitfire he had hushed with his mouth. But that was impossible now—there were people gathering, astonished to see their prince and his fiancée in deep conversation. 'I want to walk—'

'You can't walk here. We can walk back at the palace.'

'I'm sick of being cooped up.'

She was going to storm off; he knew it. Was this what the future held for the royals? Public rows on the street, drama played out wherever it suited? This mistake of his own making stared back at him. She would do it, he knew, would storm off if he insisted she return, and though he would far rather drag her into the car, he sought a rapid solution; the black moons were rising in her eyes but her pupils were dilated for battle rather than in lust this time.

'We will walk.' He had never been challenged like this, had never had anyone defy him so. He could lead an army, yet could not get her back to the car. As they stared, locked in silent battle but still smiling, he saw not just the black but the green in her eyes, and the shimmer of tears like dew in the morning and he knew where to take her. 'We will go to *verde bosco*....'

'Is that a village?' Allegra asked.

'It's not a place—' he actually smiled '—it is a forest, the foothills—it is where I go,' Alex said, and he saw her slight frown. 'When I need to get away. *Verde bosco* is where I go.'

It was the closest he'd come to admitting that at times perhaps he felt it too.

And also the reason she got in the car.

CHAPTER NINE

'WHAT the hell were you thinking?' So angry was he that for a while he said nothing else. The people watched as the couple got into the car, expecting him to turn around and speed back to the palace, sharing smiles instead when his silver car headed for the hills.

They saw it often when Alessandro was here, the low silver vehicle hugging the bends in the road—and they knew, too, that he used to ride there for hours in the rugged woods. It just hadn't happened in a long time—but now their prince was back, sharing the land he loved with his future bride.

'What were you thinking?' he demanded again.

'That I am being ignored, that I'm stuck locked away and that I wanted a few hours—'

'You are engaged to me,' Alessandro roared. 'I told you this morning that you do not just pop out, you do not go walking....' He halted then; it was safer for now to concentrate on the road, which he did, and when he heard her rapid inhale at a couple of sharper bends, he turned briefly and saw she was scared. 'I am not driving in anger,' he explained. 'I know this road well.'

So well.

He had taken it often when he had lived here, heading for the one place on Santina that soothed him. Even

GET 2 BOOKS

We'd like to send you two *Harlequin Presents®*
novels absolutely free. Accepting them puts you under
no obligation to purchase any more books.

HOW TO GET YOUR
2 FREE BOOKS AND 2 FREE GIFTS

1. Return the reply card today, and we'll send you two *Harlequin Presents* novels, absolutely free! We'll even pay the postage!

2. Accepting free books places you under no obligation to buy anything, ever. Whatever you decide, the free books and gifts are yours to keep, free!

3. We hope that after receiving your free books you'll want to remain a subscriber, but the choice is yours–to continue or cancel, any time at all!

EXTRA BONUS
You'll also get two free mystery gifts!
(worth about $10)

FREE!

▼ DETACH AND MAIL CARD TODAY! ▼

If offer card is missing, write to: The Reader Service, P.O. Box 1867, Buffalo, NY 14240-1867 or visit www.ReaderService.com

BUSINESS REPLY MAIL
FIRST-CLASS MAIL   PERMIT NO. 717   BUFFALO, NY

POSTAGE WILL BE PAID BY ADDRESSEE

THE READER SERVICE
PO BOX 1867
BUFFALO NY 14240-9952

NO POSTAGE
NECESSARY
IF MAILED
IN THE
UNITED STATES

as a child and later as an angry teenager, before he could
drive, he would ride for the day, just to get to this place.
When he could not stand the confines of the palace, when
he could not bear to breathe the stifling air, when all he
felt was oppression, it was here he would come, to a place
he could breathe, could shout if he chose, could think....

He knew how she felt, for he had felt it once too.

He pressed a button and the roof slid away. When it
was safe to do so he glanced over again and saw her more
relaxed now, eyes closed enjoying the sun and the wind
and air that was fresh.

For Allegra the silence from him was golden; she knew
he wasn't so angry now, knew that though she slept beside him every night and joined him at dinner, spoke with
him each day, really they had not been alone, had not been
themselves, since London.

She opened her eyes as the car slowed down; it was
cooler and shaded. When they came to a stop, they both
got out without a word, and she let Alex lead her to the
place he had once come to.

'I do know what it's like.' He was not shouting; he didn't
even seem cross. She was so glad for the drive, for the distance from the palace. She could see it still though, there
beneath them in the distance, but she was glad for the ex-
panse of land in between.

'Before I could drive, I used to ride here. I used to stand
here and swear I would not go back, though of course I
had to—but I promised that I would get away, that for a
few years I would live in London, live *my* life for a while,
before I returned to their ways.' They walked further into
the copse, and he showed her where he would tie his horse.
They walked further in till they were bathed in green and
they sat on the damp moss that her eyes had reminded
him of.

'We should have brought a picnic,' Allegra teased.

'I wasn't exactly planning to come here,' Alex said, but it was good to be back, to lie down on the moss and look up to the glimpses of sky that the trees soared to. To not look at her as he told her what he should not, but what she surely deserved to know. 'You know there is uproar with Sophia missing….'

'She's not missing—she's married to your friend Ash, the maharaja,' Allegra said, for when the young princess had heard that her father was about to marry her off, she had fled instead. 'But yes, there's an uproar.' Prince Rodrigruez had arrived to claim his bride, and the king had decided that Sophia's disgraced sister Carlotta would do instead. Allegra could not understand this family—how appearances rather than feelings mattered.

'There is always uproar around Sophia.' He looked up to her. 'You've heard the rumours? That she isn't…'

Allegra nodded; when he was trying to be more open, she wasn't going to play games and pretend she didn't know what he was talking about.

'My father was always strict with me, but when I was young,' he tried to recall, 'there were times we went out. There seemed more freedom then, or maybe the palace seemed bigger. Then Mother had the twins, and though my father doted on them, especially Natalia, he really wanted more sons. I know he was disappointed, and my mother… she changed.' He tried to explain. 'Maybe you would call it depression. I didn't know what it was then. But when I was twelve I knew there was going to be another baby— which should have been good news—after all, my father wanted another son. I heard them rowing—not just a row!' She looked at him. 'He told her she would bring down the monarchy—that her careless ways would cost the people dear…that her indiscretion…' He looked to the sky and could hear their voices now. 'It was not that she had an affair that upset him, he said. He was worried for the people, the damage a pregnancy—'

'No,' Allegra broke in. 'Of course he was upset.'

'You have to understand—'

'I do understand,' Allegra said, 'because I've heard those types of rows too—hundreds of them—and whatever you think of my father, he's not all that different from yours. I love him dearly, but he's a mire of double standards. If it had been my mother who had had an affair—'

'It is different,' Alex cut in. 'Since then, we must be above rumour or reproach.'

'It's hardly working though,' Allegra pointed out. 'The press are going crazy now with the goings-on. Your family are so busy trying to keep secrets that keep bursting out into the open, so busy trying to prove they're not human, when really that's all they are. Your father wasn't upset about the people—he used that as an excuse to lock her in with guilt. You won't keep me locked in, Alex.'

'You can't just wander off.'

'I promise not to come back pregnant!'

'Allegra, I'm serious. There are things that cannot be changed.' He was silent then, and they both lay still for a moment. 'Can you hear it?'

She could, the buzz of a helicopter. It might not even be for them, but then again, it may well be, yet she would not give in. 'They're here because it's such a rarity...' she attempted. 'Because they're so unused to your family doing things in a normal way. We're supposed to be engaged, we're supposed to be unable to keep our hands off each other—we should be making love in the foothills.'

'I would never compromise you like that,' Alex said.

'I know that.' She gave a small laugh. 'Shame...' And then she winced. 'I didn't mean... I wasn't trying to lead—'

'I understand,' Alex said, and he did understand, because spontaneity could not be a part of his life. And it *was* a shame. 'I would not be here if I was engaged to Anna.' She would never have fled the palace; there would have been no near row on the street. He looked over to her.

'You could have been,' Allegra said. 'You choose to live by the old rules.'

'The people knew we were rowing.'

'Of course they did,' Allegra said. 'They're not stupid.'

'It's not fitting.'

'It's a row!' Allegra shrugged. 'Couples have them all the time.'

He could hear the helicopter overhead; he had no doubt it was the paparazzi. 'Would they find us kissing?' he asked.

'I presume so,' she said. 'Had we made up.'

'Have we?'

'We're talking,' Allegra said. 'Surely that's a start. Please help me, Alex—I can't stay locked in the palace. I feel like I'm losing myself....'

'I will try,' Alex said. 'Perhaps there can be compromise.'

'I guess we've made up then.' She wanted a kiss, even if it was for the cameras; she wanted contact, wanted to feel more of him.

And he would never compromise her; she knew that, so much so that she wasn't offended when he rearranged the set, for he did it with her honour in mind. 'Pull down your dress,' he said, for it had ridden up a little. She pulled it down as far as it would go, and it felt wooden, and formal, like two actors on set, even when he spoke of logistics. 'I will move towards you.' Except it was a relief to have contact, to revisit him.

It was a duty kiss, and there was nowhere it could go.

His hand was on her waist and there it would remain; their bodies suitably apart, just their faces met. It was a gentle kiss, a reunion kiss, and all she felt were his lips and all he had were hers.

She heard the hum of the helicopter so his kiss did not deepen, and slowly he pulled back his mouth. He did not want to be prince in that moment, a normal man would be so much easier, for all he wanted was to taste her again, and he chose to.

He brushed his lips against hers and still it was gentle. It was not, though, a kiss for the cameras; it was a kiss that wished they were totally private, a kiss just for them. Both knew it even if they dared not admit it.

She could feel his breath and the increase of hers.

'Alex…' She pulled back, for it almost killed her not to roll into him. She felt his hand tighten on her waist, felt it bunch the fabric in tortured immobility. 'I don't want anything appropriate in the papers.'

'I told you. I would never compromise you. I thought you wanted us to appear normal.'

He loved kissing her—it was an entirely new sensation, and he had never been playful in his life, never.

Not once.

There was a double forbidden here.

'I don't want you accusing me of teasing.'

'I know that.'

'And we can't do anything that might look…'

He knew that too.

'Just kiss,' Alex said. Maybe it tastes so sweet because it is forbidden, he thought, because there is nothing more they could do. Maybe it had simply been too long without a woman; he could not allow himself to entertain that it was solely for her, for more of her, that he lowered his head again.

And a kiss without contact was torture.

A delicious torture as their mouths met again.

Torture to not be able to roam his body, to not accept him, for she knew he was wild to press into her. To not be able to forget about cameras, Santina and the predicament they were in. Yet torture to forget these things, too, as mouths mingled.

She could feel her breath quicken, her mouth open to take him, except he pulled back. She gave a reluctant moan and wanted to take it back, for she was not supposed to be enjoying it so, but then so, too, did he.

It was the most erotic of moments, a seemingly chaste kiss but with bodies that were flaming.

The helicopter buzzed louder, like the nerves between her legs, and they *had* to keep it tasteful, so he lifted his head and showered her face with small kisses. He smiled down at her, and even in his arms, she could not tell of her pleasure, and even in hers he could not admit to the same.

'If you weren't a prince…' Allegra looked up at him, and then she stopped, because she would now be teasing. For tonight they would be alone again, and she could not succumb, could not give that part of herself and still come out of this sane.

'I *am* one,' he said, for he could never forget.

Except were he not a prince, his hand would be between her legs now, she would be writhing on the moss and his face would be over hers, his body too.

But at least he could kiss her.

Her breasts ached for his hands; her body begged for his weight. There was a purr in her mouth that must have dictated her want, for his breathing was ragged and so, too, was hers. But Alex was right, there *were* limits.

'We should go back.'

She pulled her lips away, dared not admit to the heat

in her body, or that if he kissed her further she would surely come.

'Of course.' He was back to being prince, though his thoughts were the same. 'I think they would have got their shot by now.'

It did not sting to hear his cold words; they were actually welcome, for she needed a reality check.

It was a different drive back to the palace. He showed her the landmarks, the little blue flowers that dotted the hills. She showed him the flowers the girl had given her in the café.

'They're what a little girl gave me.' She picked them up from the concourse, but they were fading fast. 'They need water.'

'They are everywhere,' Alex said. 'They are exclusive to Santina, they flower all year. Really, they are a common weed—we have trouble controlling them.'

'I think they're beautiful,' Allegra said and Alex screwed up his nose.

It was a more relaxed couple that arrived back at the palace. It actually didn't feel strange to walk through the palace holding hands.

She felt rumpled and a bit grubby, but she felt the most normal she had in ages, buoyed from fresh air and company, from his kiss, from their talk. It was impossible not to smile.

Until they were immediately summoned to the king's study. He stood stern and visibly angry, but the queen gave a tentative smile. 'Allegra.' The queen was kind. 'We have been so worried—anything could have happened.'

'Nothing did.'

'You might have been recognised.'

'I *was* recognised.' Allegra was trying not to be rude to the queen. 'I walked into a café and do you know what the owner did? He shut the shop—he let all the people who were currently there stay, but he allowed no one else in, and the people were delightful. They were absolutely thrilled and they let me be. Apart from one little girl.' She looked at their uncomprehending faces, and her mind spun in circles—could they not understand how nice and simple it had been, that a little girl had come and given her a bunch of flowers?

She showed the wilting bunch, but the king just huffed. 'Weeds…'

She told them that she had walked into shops, and that she had made their day, and she looked to the queen. 'I am a poor substitute for you, but they were thrilled. I shopped, and if people approached, it was just to say hello.'

The king, unbidden, reached for her bags. 'Tomorrow the papers will be full of the gifts, of the royals' greed….'

'Leave her things,' Alex snapped, but the king ignored his son's orders and opened the bags. 'Have someone go now and pay—'

'I paid,' Allegra said. 'Of course I paid.' And maybe the king was expecting pearls and jewels to spill from the bags that he shook out on the desk, but it was a few post-cards and a couple of souvenirs from Santina and a little snow globe with a tiny castle inside.

That they would do that, take her things and just riffle through them, was too much for Allegra. She would say something rude—but she must not. If she opened her mouth now she would be disrespectful to the king. Whatever they thought of her father, he had taught her better than they knew, so instead just a sob of frustration came from her lips as she fled the room.

'Go after her,' the queen said to her son, and then turned to her husband. 'Eduardo, you should not have touched her things.'

But he did not go after; he faced his father.

'You say the people love her, and yet you try to change her!'

'I rule Santina.' The king picked up the book he had been reading, the book that had caused Allegra's family so much shame. 'You lose your head to her and you will make poor decisions—you will turn this family into a circus. Do you want this for your people? She will act accordingly.'

'She just went for a walk, for God's sake!' The queen's voice was rising. 'She just went for a walk…'

'That's how it starts.' The king turned to his wife, to the woman he had once trusted. 'And then she makes friends, and then she makes closer friends and before you know it…' He looked to his wife. 'The rules are in place for a reason. We are not changing our ways to accommodate your fiancée, Alessandro. It is she who must change hers. When I am dead and gone, you can do what you see fit, but while I rule…' He looked to his son, to his eldest, to the strongest and wisest of his children, and he would not allow him to give in as he once had, would not allow him to open up to the hurt he would feel. As his son strode out of the study, the king hurled the truth to his back and watched it stiffen. 'I am still your king.'

It was a cauldron, an impossible one, and soon enough it had to explode.

CHAPTER TEN

'ALLEGRA.' It was the next morning when he crawled into bed, ten minutes before the maids appeared. It was all he could take—twenty minutes simply killed him and last night he had chosen the sofa. Her eyes were still swollen from crying, for despite his words in the woods, last night he had made it clear—there could be no major changes, just the occasional compromise.

'What?' It was a surly response.

'Stop sulking.'

'I'm not,' she said. 'I'm thinking.'

'About…'

'How impossible this is. How I want to go home.' She turned to him. 'You're going to London soon…can't I at least join you?'

She couldn't—yes, he had work to do in London, but he also had plans and certainly he did not want her around to spoil them.

'To see my family…' There was so much going on, and all she got were glimpses. It was as if she were being cut off even from them. 'I hardly hear from them. I want to see them, talk to them….'

Which was the last thing he could risk. She trusted them implicitly, she defended them at every turn, yet more and more they were becoming entwined with his—her sister

Izzy and his brother, Matteo, were holed up somewhere together, and his cousin Rafe McFarland had married her stepsister.

He could not risk her confiding in them, and must, as his father had pointed out, keep her removed from their scandal.

'You have things to do here.'

'I'm dying here,' Allegra said.

'Stop with the dramatics. You keep insisting you are busy with your book.' There was an aggrieved note to his voice, for her book kept her up late each night, her book made sure he was asleep on the damned sofa by the time she came to bed. Still they could not discuss things further, for the door knocked and Alex called for the maid to enter.

'Just coffee?' Allegra frowned when they pretended to wake after the maid had brought in the trolley. 'Where's breakfast?'

'You didn't take too long to adjust to the lifestyle.' Alex smirked. 'My parents have asked that we join them for breakfast—they want to go over wedding plans. You still need to select a designer for your gown.'

'It seems rather a waste,' Allegra said. 'Given we're both hoping I shan't be wearing it—and anyway,' she admitted, 'there's nothing for me to select, they're all the same.' She heard the whine in her voice and halted herself. Had it really come to this, sitting up in bed with the most beautiful view on God's earth, next to the most stunning man, and complaining about designers? Over and over she had to check herself, tell herself she had nothing to complain about—it was just that she missed him. Missed the man she had met in London so very much, missed the glimpse of the dream.

'Why breakfast?' Allegra asked, because it was all so

formal. Why did this family have to arrange a simple conversation?

'Because my father has commitments all day and I am flying out tonight.'

'And I'm stuck here…' There was that whine again, and even she couldn't bear to hear it, so she put down her cup and climbed out of bed, lay in the bath that the maid had run and tried to calm down, tried not to think of the real reason for his regular jaunts to London—as if a man like Alex would sleep alone for long.

Breakfast was excruciating, from the moment she sat down and selected her favourite croissant.

'Actually,' Zoe said as Allegra smeared strawberry jam over it. 'I've had a word with the chefs and they're going be preparing a light selection for you, Allegra.'

'Excuse me?'

'In preparation for the wedding.'

'You think I need to lose weight?' She waited for Zoe to retract from the mild confrontation, but instead the queen just smiled.

'You have put a little on.'

Allegra couldn't believe her ears. She was slim, always had been. Her father was forever telling her she needed to put weight on.

'Leave it,' Alex said, thankfully to the queen and not to Allegra.

'I'm just trying to help. You know the pressure she's going to be under—the people expect perfection. I don't want Allegra feeling awkward on the day. It's hard for her, I realise that—she has sudden twenty-four-hour access to top class chefs…. I'm just suggesting that, before it becomes an issue, she nip things in the bud.'

'Well, don't.' Alex's voice was loaded with warning, as, too, was the look that he shot his mother. His eyes, though, were surprisingly kind when they turned to her. 'Ignore that,' he said. 'Just completely dismiss it—you look wonderful.' His eyes held hers and she wished for the hundredth time that he meant it, that the public facade was real.

'You need to choose a designer for your dress.' Zoe didn't exactly change the subject, but at least she moved away from Allegra's waistline.

'I know... I just...' She hated all the suggestions, hated them because they were all just a slightly different version of the same. She'd been told, too, to grow out her fringe so that she could wear a more traditional hairstyle. 'I've got a couple more to see this week. What about you?' Allegra asked her fiancé, who was clearly bored senseless by the conversation.

'I'll be wearing military uniform.' He looked at her non-comprehending face. 'I did several years' service, and given it is our family the soldiers serve...' He didn't even bother finishing his sentence, just picked up his ringing phone and carried on a brief conversation.

'That's extremely rude, Alessandro.' The king looked up from his newspaper.

'That call was urgent,' Alessandro responded. 'I've been trying to get hold of someone for two weeks. Belinda was just letting me know that he has accepted an invitation to dinner tomorrow night.'

'It could have waited,' barked the king.

'Somehow I don't think His Royal Highness Sheikh Razim Abdullah likes to be kept waiting.' Alex could out snob anyone, Allegra noted, even his own father. 'Given he is considering buying my business, it seemed prudent to tell Belinda to let him know that tomorrow we would be delighted to join him.'

Allegra's eyes shot to his as she heard the 'we,' but perhaps he realised his mistake, for he did not return her gaze. Instead he took great interest in a bowl of raw sugar cubes, selecting one and then another for his coffee.

'How are your parents?' Zoe must have felt the sudden drop in temperature because she moved the conversation on quickly.

'They're fine, thank you.' Allegra could hardly breathe, but she did her best to be polite. 'I spoke with my father yesterday.' She turned and forced a smile at the queen. 'He's looking forward to seeing Alex when he's over—'

'I shall be working,' Alex said.

'He also asked after you, Your Highness.'

'Oh.'

'You mentioned you might be visiting London too….' Allegra tried to recall the conversation she had had with the queen the other night.

'Just a fleeting visit.' Zoe gave a tight smile. 'Formal.'

'You could pop in for a cup of tea!' The king thought this highly amusing and Allegra really couldn't take it much more. She hated the lot of them.

'Excuse me.' She put down her napkin. 'I need to get ready to speak with the next designer.' She looked to Alessandro. 'Could I have a quick word?' She was very close to crying. 'I'd like your opinion on something.'

She waited till they were in the bedroom and well out of earshot to pick up the conversation where she had left off.

'Because heaven help me if I formed an opinion on my own!'

'Allegra.' He was completely bored with her. 'I don't have time for this. What did you want to speak with me about?'

'Why are they so rude? What's so bloody funny about my father inviting them over that your father can be so rude?'

He merely shrugged, and she moved on to the other

thing that was killing her, the other thing she simply had to know. 'You're going out with Belinda tomorrow night.' He had the audacity to roll his eyes. 'And don't even try saying it's business.'

'I told you and I have told my parents and I am sick of saying it—I don't run a market stall, I don't make a living from reality TV shows. I employ over two hundred people and if I don't dispose of my business interests correctly then that is two hundred people who could be out of work. And yes, Belinda will be joining me for dinner, because it is a business dinner, because the sheikh will be bringing his assistant too.'

'So you've never slept with her.' Allegra knew that he had—she knew, just the way a woman did, from seeing how Belinda looked at him, from the little laughs that wafted over on Skype conversations, that she was so much more than just a PA. 'You really expect me to believe—'

'Of course I've slept with her.' He didn't seem to see what the problem was. 'But I haven't since our engagement—I have to keep up the happy little charade.' He did nothing to soothe her, nothing to comfort her. 'Now, if you'll excuse me, I'm going to my office. You carry on talking weddings....'

'Screw you!'

'Oh, but you won't,' Alex said. 'Hell...' he cussed out. 'The one respite we could have during this torture, the one piece of pleasure we could share, and you've bolted your knees together.' He saw her lips tighten and the two dots of colour burning on her cheeks. Then with a sob she fled.

He called to a maid, had her bring him some more crystals and water, but antacids were no longer working. There was a constant burn in his gut, and though he never went after a woman when she stormed off, this time he did, for he was not proud of his words and he wanted to apologise for them.

* * *

She wasn't in their suite, nor back in her little turret, nor did he find her in the kitchen, the place he had found her after their last row. But finally he found her out at the stables, still fizzing with anger, and she was heaving a saddle onto an equally temperamental mare.

'What on earth are you doing?'

She didn't bother to answer.

'She's not suitable for riding....'

'You ride her,' Allegra said.

'I know how!'

He dismissed the worried-looking stable boy with a flick of his wrist.

'He did warn me,' Allegra said, 'so don't bite his head off later.'

'You cannot ride her.'

'I want to,' Allegra said. 'Anyway, I need the exercise apparently.'

She mounted the horse and felt the power beneath her, and even if she didn't feel quite so brave now, she refused to show it.

'Allegra, you are being ridiculous—this could be dangerous.'

'I've had riding lessons,' she called over her shoulder as she trotted across the yard. 'My father—'

'This is not some docile mare from the local pony club that your father had you join, so he could flirt with the mothers....'

He was loathsome, so loathsome she kicked off, and just tried to concentrate on staying on, because this was a huge powerful beast she was riding, and he was right, this wasn't some little pony she had trotted around a ring on. She couldn't see for her tears, couldn't think for her anger, she just wanted speed and space. And she wanted him to come after her, she admitted with a sob; she wanted him to be with her in this, to be the man she had thought he was.

Suddenly she lost her footing in the stirrup; she sailed through the air and collided with the grassy floor. Her landing didn't actually hurt that much, for she was in agony already, but she felt the thud to her head, and goodness it was a relief to cry, to lie on the grass as he ran over, not to have to hide her tears.

'Lie still.' He was incredibly calm. 'Where does it hurt?'

'I don't know.'

'Did you hit your head?' His fingers examined her; there was a large lump forming on her forehead that was worrisome and his fingers worked their way down her body, a slow perusal as he checked for anything obvious. He expected her to wince or call out in pain, but she just lay there crying.

'Nothing seems broken.' She looked up to him and maybe he had had a fright after all, because he was actually sweating. Or maybe that was more from the rapid ride over to collect his casualty. 'You have a nasty lump on your head though.'

'Sorry…' She looked up but there were three of him, all swimming around. She'd been nothing but trouble, she knew that—he was as trapped as she.

'You've nothing to be sorry for.'

Oh, but she did. She turned her head and was sick into the grass, more embarrassed than she had ever been in her life to be seen like this. 'I should have just broken my neck, then you could have been a poor widower.'

'Allegra…'

'Then you wouldn't have had to marry. You could just sleep with everyone and behave as horribly as you like and they'd say, "But poor Alessandro, who can blame him?"'

'Allegra.' He was very, very calm and she knew she was rambling. 'You have a head injury.'

'Thanks to you.' She was cross-eyed trying to look at him. 'You just let me ride off.' It was the most stupid thing to say, but she was past caring, lying on the grass, slurring her words. 'I could have been miles away….'

'Had I chased you she would have just gone faster—she'd have thought it was a race.' She had no idea the fear that had gripped him as she had ridden off, to stand and watch helplessly as she jumped onto the most temperamental mare. He had come to apologise but instead he had had no choice but to stand and watch the inevitable, to see her tumble. 'Your stomach…' He had not checked it, he was not a doctor, but the thought of a hoof kicking her actually made him feel sick. He was vaguely aware of activity behind him and he shouted orders, called for the doctor to meet them back at the palace and then he turned and spoke gently to her. 'Let's get you back home.'

'It doesn't feel like home though.' There was the indignity of being placed on a golf buggy and driven back to the palace and then a very shaky walk up the stairs.

'I'll carry you,' he offered, but for some reason that just upset her even more.

'You can leave me now.'

'Not yet,' Alessandro said. 'The doctor wants to see you.' He shooed out the maid, because he knew that she hated to be fussed over, and then started to pull at her boots as she attempted her buttons.

'I can manage,' Allegra said.

He was not remotely impressed. 'Believe me, I am getting no kicks out of this,' he said, and that eked a smile. 'There's no perverse pleasure in taking your vomit-stained blouse off.' He picked up the lace nightdress and it was clearly too complicated so he went to a drawer and pulled out one of his T-shirts instead. Even though it must have been laundered to the strict palace guidelines, still she was sure that she caught the scent of him as he slid it over her head.

'Bed.' He pulled the sheets back and she climbed in; her brain seemed to be thumping away at her skull as he opened the door and let the old doctor in. He examined her very thoroughly and she could smell his horrible breath as he shone a light in both eyes then spoke in deep tones to Alex. She heard the words *commozione cerebrale* and if she hadn't been lying down she would have fainted, but then Alex looked over and gave her a smile.

'That's "concussion" to you!' He smiled at her melo-drama and then thanked the doctor. Left alone he sat on her bed. 'You have to rest for a couple of days—there will be a nurse to come in and check you hourly throughout the day and night.'

'Is it really necessary?'

'Apparently.'

Allegra woke a little later. The flowers the little girl had given her in the café yesterday had been placed in a small vase by the bed and they had perked up with the water, the blue petals like tiny stars. She gazed on them slowly, re-playing the day's events, awareness creeping in that Alex was in the room too. She looked over to where he sat in an armchair dozing—just as beautiful as ever. And even though they were planning a wedding, he was still just as unattainable as ever. She could never have his heart—he had told her the day they met that he didn't do love, that it simply wouldn't happen with him, but it was hard to finally accept it. The nurse came in and took her blood pressure and shone the little light in her eyes and then left them alone.

'I'm alive apparently,' she said as his dark eyes peeked open. She was terribly embarrassed, could sort of remember the stupid things that she'd said out on the field to him, tried to remember if she'd declared undying love or anything equally awful.

'I'm sorry if I made a fool of myself.'

'Stop apologising.'

'I can't actually remember what I said.'

'Something about what a merry widower I'd make.'

'You're supposed to be in London.'

'It doesn't matter.'

'What about Sheikh...' She couldn't remember his name.

'He's a family man—he understood completely when he heard you had had an accident. He sends his best wishes for a speedy return to full health.'

'I'm fine.'

'No,' Alex said, 'you're not. It's not just the fall.' He put on a side light and looked over to where she lay and even if her fringe mainly hid them, there was so much trouble in her eyes. 'When I met you that day—'

'Don't.' She closed her eyes, didn't want to hear how she hadn't lived up to expectations, how he could never have guessed the trouble he was taking on. 'I was boring till I met you.' She opened her eyes and saw that he was smiling.

'I doubt that.'

'Honestly!' She blinked. 'I'm the quiet one in my family.'

'It must get pretty noisy around Christmas.'

'It does,' Allegra said, thinking of the wonderful times she'd had with her family, the rows and the singalongs, the parties and the whole drama that was part and parcel of being a Jackson. 'I can't stand to hear your parents being derisive about them, that it's such a joke that my father might invite—'

'There I must defend them.' He came over and sat on the edge of the bed. 'I know they can be unforgivably rude about your family, my father especially, but that reference to dropping in for tea this morning had nothing to do with you, or anything derisive about your family. It was aimed entirely at my mother.' He saw her frown. 'She had tea with your father apparently.'

'She did.' Allegra nodded. 'My father got lost the morning after the party....' Her mouth gaped open. 'He's jealous!'

'Not jealous...' Alex said, and then thought some more. 'Perhaps.'

'It was innocent.'

'Of course,' Alex agreed, and thought some more. 'Maybe you are right about my parents, maybe my father was hurt more than he admitted about her indiscretion.'

'Maybe he should tell her then.'

Alex shook his head. 'That will never happen.' He looked at her fringe and he wanted to see her eyes so he brushed it aside and winced at the large bruise. 'Your hair is too long.'

'I'm to grow out my fringe apparently.' She gave a tight smile. 'They want a more classical look for the wedding.' And then she smiled a bit wider. 'I can't believe your dad's upset by my father and your mum. I wish you knew my dad... I wish I could see him.'

'I'm sorry that you miss them.'

'I hear everything third-hand—Angel's married your cousin.'

Alex smiled. 'It was a very quick wedding.'

'But even so, there's my brother Ben and Natalia, my sister Ella and Hassan. She's pregnant, and—' All she did was hear about things when she wanted to live them. 'I know you don't understand but I miss them, I love them....'

'I know you do,' Alex said, but no, he didn't understand.

He was actually wonderful company; if you had to spend two days in bed with a thumping headache then Alex made a surprisingly good nurse. His complete ease with silence was soothing, and he was so sparse with words—at least she wasn't asked how she was feeling every ten minutes. He just told her she'd live when she moaned about her headache, or looked up from his computer when she staggered to the bathroom.

But late one afternoon, she returned from a bath run by the maid, dressed now in her Santina lace nightdress, and slipped into freshly laundered sheets. She closed her eyes, exhausted from the simple effort and then suddenly opened them again.

'Has Angel rung?'

'I spoke to her this morning,' Alex said. 'And your father too. I've been keeping them updated on your progress.'

'What about Izzy?'

'I have spoken to her too.' He glanced over. 'She's still here in Santina, staying at the palazzo with my brother, Matteo.'

'And she hasn't been to see me...' Allegra reached for her phone, craving the company of her sister, but Alex came over to the bed. 'I told her you were resting.'

'Well, I'm awake now.'

'Allegra.' He took the phone from her hand and put it on the bedside. 'At the moment you are upset... Wouldn't it be hard not to tell the truth to Izzy if you saw her?'

'Izzy would never tell.'

'She would not tell your brother Leo?' He watched as she frowned. 'It would seem that Leo is now seeing Anna, my ex-fiancée. Allegra, do you understand you cannot speak with your family as you once did?' He saw a glare of defiance and chose to quickly change track. 'As I said, I was speaking with Izzy and I'm sure you're not aware, but Matteo organises a charity concert once a year, out at the amphitheatre. One of Izzy's songs has been billed….'

'Izzy's singing?' Allegra's eyes narrowed. She'd heard his family's reaction when Izzy had attempted to sing at the engagement party. She wouldn't put it past them at all to have her up onstage in front of a huge audience, just for the cheap laugh they might get.

'No.' Alex shook his head. 'But her song will be played and she is going to be watching in the wings. I said that we would attend. It will be nice for you to get out. I know you feel cooped up.' He gave her hand a little squeeze. 'Something perhaps to look forward to.'

'I just miss everyone,' Allegra admitted. 'I feel as if I've dropped off the face of the earth and that no one's actually noticed, that no one even cares.'

'Come here.' He stood and she frowned up at him. 'I want to show you something.' He pulled her pashmina from the chair and wrapped it around her shoulders, and then took her elbow and led her, a bit wobbly, out of the room, down a long corridor and then down a flight of stairs to a vast set of French windows. 'Do you still think no one cares?'

She looked out to the entrance of the palace where there were hundreds and hundreds of flowers laid at the palace gates. Some of the bouquets were formal, but there were also hundreds of posies of little blue stars and it was those that meant the most. 'They're for you,' Alex told her. 'The people heard you'd had a fall and they have been bring-ing them for the past two days. There are bouquets being delivered hourly—they are down in the drawing room, in the dining room—'

'For me?'

'We've never seen anything like it,' Alessandro admitted. 'The papers did not exaggerate or lie—our people really do love you.'

And it helped, it really did help, made the madness of the situation just a touch more bearable, but as she headed back to bed, he gave her a thin smile. 'I am heading to London. I've been putting it off, but now that you're feeling better... It'll just be for a couple of weeks, I'll be back for the concert.'

'Weeks?'

'There is a lot to be done and I cannot put off Razim again.'

So he would be out tomorrow night with Belinda. And she didn't have the excuse of a *commozione cerebrale*. She had no choice but to lie there and hold on to her feelings, but as he stood he gave her shoulder a brotherly squeeze and then left her. She almost heard the sigh of relief as he closed the bedroom door behind him.

Well, what did she expect? Allegra thought as she lay there. Of course he'd be on the first flight out.

The people might love her; it was the prince who seemed to find it impossible to.

CHAPTER ELEVEN

SHE couldn't go out while he was away—not because of the strict orders from the palace, more because of the egg on her forehead. So she mooched around the palace, trying not to imagine him out with the hard-nailed Belinda. She rang Izzy, but just got her voice mail, and Angel wasn't responding to her emails either. Allegra looked up when the maid knocked on her door.

'Raymondo is here.'

'Raymond!' corrected a loud, rather effeminate voice. She was so bored looking at wedding dresses, especially when she had no intention of even wearing it. She had to really make an effort to look enthusiastic as Raymond walked in and she waited, waited for the entourage behind him, for the swatches of white fabric, but all it was was him, not even a sketch pad.

'They always do that,' he said by way of introduction. 'They think it makes me sound more exotic!' He was from London too, and she nearly fell on his neck at the sound of his familiar accent. 'So, let's get started. What are your thoughts?' he asked. She drew in a breath, ready to give the appropriate answer when Raymond cut it. 'Actually, I've already been briefed. White Santina lace, yawn, yawn…'

Was it wrong that she giggled?

'In at the waist, full skirt, long train…' He rolled his

eyes and perhaps saw the sparkle of tears in hers. 'It's your wedding day, my dear—' he handed her a tissue '—I promise I will make you look beautiful.'

'I know.' Allegra sniffed. 'Sorry, I don't know what's wrong with me.' She tapped her forehead, tried to blame it on the bruise.

'Maybe you're just marrying the Crown Prince of Santina,' Raymond said wisely. 'It must be the most terrible pressure for an ordinary girl.' And he said *ordinary* so nicely, in a completely different way to Alex, but there was that word again, and along with it more tears.

'You know there are two dresses,' Raymond said. 'One as a backup in case my innovative white Santina lace in-at-the-waist dress design is leaked out.'

He did make her smile. 'I don't think they'd want me wearing anything that might remotely surprise.'

'I still have to make an alternative though,' Raymond pointed out. 'It might make the fittings more fun. What if you could have exactly the dress you wanted…?'

She'd never really thought.

'Think about it,' he said. 'What if you could have your perfect dress?'

'I don't know…' There was a germ of an idea, but she brushed it off; she certainly wasn't going to reveal it to him.

'A good designer is as confidential as a doctor, and,' Raymond added, 'I don't write anything down—you simply tell me your dreams and I create them.'

Was it sad that Raymond was the highlight of her days, especially with Alex away? She loved his visits, loved chatting to him, and as her bruise faded, so too did her reserve. She would stand in the bedroom being measured and fitted and then, when his assistant would walk off with tissue paper and plans, she would tell him her dreams, closing her eyes and imagining walking down the aisle to a husband that loved her, in the dress of her dreams.

'It's going to be stunning,' Raymond said. 'And I'm going to be making a start on it tonight—I can't wait. You've got the concert tonight.'

'I do.'

Her heart was fluttering with excitement, energised from Raymond's visit and Alex had rung to say he was on his way home and tonight she would finally see Izzy.

'What are you wearing?' Raymond asked.

She sighed and pulled out a pale linen dress with a fitted light jacket over the top. She wasn't remotely offended when he screwed up his nose. 'I'm wearing heels there, but I'm bringing pumps to change into.'

'It's a rock concert,' Raymond said.

'I know.'

'Come on, you!'

'Where are we going?'

'Shopping, of course.'

'I can't…' She thought of the last time she'd left the building unannounced, but Raymond wasn't remotely perturbed.

'I'll ring ahead to the boutiques. You're out shopping with your designer, what else is a princess-to-be supposed to be doing?'

'Can we stop for coffee?' Allegra asked.

'Absolutely.' Raymond smiled. 'And cake!'

They did, and it was the most wonderful day—spent shopping and laughing and then, laden with bags, they stopped at what was now Allegra's favourite café, though this time the car waited outside.

Again the owner closed up the shop.

'I hope it doesn't affect his trade,' Allegra said after they had placed their orders.

'Rubbish!' Raymond said. 'It will have multiplied it—everyone will want to eat and drink here, knowing this is where the future princess chooses to come.' He gave her a pensive smile and then he told her more about himself, about the boyfriend who had broken his heart and now wanted to get back with him. What a pleasure it was actually to sit and listen, to hear about his problems instead of focusing on hers.

'Maybe he's realised he loves you,' Allegra offered.

'I'm on the verge of being famous!' Raymond said. 'Thanks to designing your gown. Fernando always accused me of being a bit boring, that my designs did not make enough money.' He looked to Allegra. 'Now he's decided that he misses me—I want to believe he loves *me*, not the glamorous new version.'

He spoke to her heart and she understood.

'I want him to love the real me.'

It played in her head, over and over, as she arrived back at the palace.

She changed into clothes that were far, far more expensive than her old life would have permitted, but the style was one she had once worn.

She was dressed and ready and unbelievably nervous as she went downstairs to wait for Alex to get home, before they headed out to the concert.

'Allegra!' The queen gave her a lovely smile. 'Shouldn't you be getting ready? Alessandro's driver just informed us he'll be here in a moment and then it will be straight to the helicopter.'

'I am changed.' Allegra swallowed.

'You're wearing jeans!'

'And boots,' Allegra said. 'Aren't they divine?' They were, the leather as soft as butter; they were so perfect, so wonderful, that she wanted to name them.

'Your father…' A maid handed her the telephone and Allegra grabbed at it like a lifeline. He'd hardly called in weeks, and whenever she did he was invariably out, but it was such a relief to hear his voice.

'How are you?'

'Great!' Allegra said. 'I haven't heard from you. Why are you ringing me on this phone?' She knew Alex had arrived, but it had been ages since she had spoken to her father so she moved to another room to continue the conversation.

'I thought that was what I was supposed to do,' Bobby said. 'Cheaper than a mobile…' He tried to make a joke except Allegra didn't smile. 'Anyway, you'd have lots to be getting on with, I don't want to get in your way.'

'You don't.'

'Have you seen Izzy?'

'I'm seeing her tonight!' She was so looking forward to it, even if she would only get a bit of time with her at the after party, but she couldn't wait to talk to her.

'I just wanted to check something with you, Allegra. I've been offered a job—it's a regular spot, on a sports quiz show. The money's good and it keeps my face out there….'

'Sounds great, Dad.' Allegra grinned. It was the perfect job for her father; he loved the spotlight and attention. 'So what did you want to check?' Occasionally he asked her to look through a contract before he signed it, but she frowned as her father answered.

'Well, will it make things awkward for you?'

'How could it make things awkward?'

'I just….' She could hear her father's discomfort. 'I don't want to do anything that might embarrass you, like I did with the speech.'

'Dad!'

'And I won't talk about you on the television or any-thing or in the press.'

'I know that.'

'Well, I just want to make sure I'm doing the right thing.' He said goodbye, but somehow it was awkward.

Alex got to the foyer in time to hear his father scolding the maid for giving Allegra the phone.

'It's her father calling,' Alex pointed out.

'And she's about to go out on an official function—he's been told not to ring for a chat.' The king bristled. 'I'm going to have Antonio have another word with him—and you need to speak with her,' the king said. 'Properly this time. She's not to drop everything when one of her blasted family calls—she needs to be away from their influence. Is it any wonder she's going out dressed like a delinquent teenager, with their poor influence?'

Allegra walked in then and Alex saw she looked hardly like a delinquent teenager, just more like the woman he had first met. London had not been as he'd expected, in fact. All too often he had found himself sitting in the bar where they had met, or walking near her small flat, try-ing to fathom how he could make up for so drastically changing someone's life—for despite trying to deny it, despite perhaps not understanding it, he knew she had been happy then.

'Allegra.' He gave her a kiss as she walked in, but it was a tired kiss, a weary kiss, and for a moment he held her because he was not looking forward to what he had to say—to tell her in no uncertain terms that she needed to remove herself further from her family. He needed to think, needed some time to work out a better solution, except time seemed to be running away. The date for the wedding would be announced tomorrow and sooner than she knew it the day would be here.

Allegra blinked in surprise when she saw him. He was dressed in his suit, just as he so often did, but he must have missed shaving this morning, for he was the most unkempt she had ever seen him—his black hair tousled, looking so drained, so tired—and she almost felt sorry for him, for the last thing it looked like he needed was a rock concert.

'Allegra's wearing jeans,' Zoe said, waiting for some sort of reaction. 'Alessandro, are you going to get changed?' He completely ignored her.

'Come on,' he said to Allegra, 'the chopper's waiting. This thing is timed down to the last second—Matteo has asked that we not be late.'

'Well, at least put on your tie,' Zoe called as he took Allegra's hand.

'It's a rock concert,' he said.

'And you're a prince.'

'Which means I'll be the only idiot wearing a suit.'

As they walked to the helipad, he asked, 'How have you been? Your bruise is gone.'

'I'm much better thanks.' She gave him a smile. 'I feel a bit more myself.'

'You look it.' She wasn't sure if it was a reference to her jeans, but there was no barb in his words; it was as if all the energy had gone out of him.

'Are you okay?'

'I will be,' he said. 'It's just been a tough couple of weeks.'

There was no chance to talk further, the whir of the chopper was already chasing away their words. Instead they sat in silence for the short ride to the amphitheatre, Alex staring out through the glass. She could not fathom his thinking, wondered perhaps if he was missing Belinda, or just his life back in London, if seeing his fiancée at a charity concert was perhaps the last place he wanted to be. All the excitement just oozed out of her.

The helicopter touched down. The rest of the crowd had been there all day, with the Crown Prince and his fiancée arriving to enjoy the evening section. But instead of being amongst them, they were moved to the front, to a box surrounded by bodyguards.

And cameras flashed, not for five minutes, not for ten, but as the sun lowered and the sky darkened, the cameras continued and Allegra felt so exposed, because at any second someone in the crowd was taking her picture. Alex knew too, for every now and then he would smile and move his head to speak to her, but not once did he touch her. Apart from the walk from the helicopter where he had briefly held her hand, there had been no contact.

There was the most romantic song playing, she was sitting in the amphitheatre with her prince, the people surrounding them delighted by their presence, the whole place full of love, and never had Allegra felt lonelier. She had missed Alex so much, had looked forward to this night and ridiculously so, but now that it was here, it just rammed home the lack of love.

'What was that?' Alex leant forward and spoke to one of his aides. 'There's a change in the programme….' Allegra could not care less; she just wanted the night over. She was sick of sitting, smiling and pretending to be having the time of her life, was sick of being with a man who felt so little for her. 'Your sister is singing.'

And she could not smile, for she felt sick, absolutely sick to her stomach, that the Santinas would stoop so low.

'So she can be publicly ridiculed this time!' She wanted to dash over there, to warn Izzy, to tell her that this was the nail in the coffin, that she was being used just to confirm the Jacksons' unsuitability; she cringed for her sister, how they had all been so derisive at the party.

'I had nothing to do with this,' Alex said.

And it was too late to do anything, Allegra realised. It had been too late since the day she met Alex in the bar and she had been naive enough to think that she could handle this.

There was Izzy, stepping nervous and shy onto the stage dressed in her trademark platform shoes, wearing impossibly short shorts. She looked beautiful to Allegra; she *was* beautiful, but she could just guess as to the palace's reaction.

She watched as her sister took to the piano and offered a silent prayer—she knew Izzy could sing, but there had been sound engineers on that awful reality show. Now it was just her, unrehearsed too. Allegra felt sick to her stomach for her sister, except as the piano played, as Izzy started to sing, Allegra's nerves for her sister faded. She realised she was hearing her true voice—away from the engineers and recording studio, away from people trying to make her conform. Tonight she heard the real Izzy for the first time—and yes, a star was born.

Her voice was like liquid heaven; it filled the amphitheatre and silenced the crowd. Even the cameras that had been trained on Allegra and Alessandro stopped. Izzy was centre stage and this truly was her moment, the crowd holding up their glow sticks. Allegra felt goose bumps as she watched her sister, her little sister, grow up in a moment, watched her shine, watched as her eyes glanced for assurance, not to the royal area, not to her big sister, but to the wing. She was singing for someone and it had to be Matteo. Suddenly Allegra wanted to cry, but she dared not, and she wanted to turn, to tell Alessandro that his plan had backfired, but she was too moved, too lost in the song.

Look at me, I'm not who you see...

Deep inside there's someone else, longing to break free...

She just had, Allegra realised. Izzy had broken free, and though the words seemed aimed at Allegra's heart, from Izzy's shy glances to the side of the stage, from the love that blazed in her eyes, she knew that the words were intended for another.

Alex could feel Allegra beside him as he watched the woman they had all scorned prove so many people wrong.

He wanted to take Allegra's hand, wanted to relax and absorb the moment, but he was sitting next to a woman who loathed the palace, who did not want to be queen, who wanted this duty over.

He looked over to her glassy eyes, heard a tiny sniff. How he wanted to comfort her, to be proud with her, but he couldn't give up his right to the throne. He couldn't.

If he walked away it fell to Matteo.

Matteo was tough, completely capable, but... Alex looked to Izzy, heard the pure talent, a talent that would be silenced. Did Allegra not see what might happen here?

'She was amazing!' Allegra turned to him, but his face was rigid. She did not get this man. Did nothing move him? Was he so embalmed in royal blood that a glorious voice in such a magnificent place could leave him still as cold as the marble statues back at the palace?

'I'd like to see Izzy...' Allegra said. 'Can we go back-stage?'

'I rather think your sister is busy,' Alex said. 'Perhaps we should leave them to it.'

She'd had so much pinned on tonight, had ridiculously got her hopes up, but she couldn't keep up appearances any longer. The flash of the cameras flooded the blacked-out car as they drove back to the palace and she felt Alex's eyes on her.

'Can the tears wait till we get back to the palace at least?'

'Oh, let them see them, maybe they'll report that cracks are starting to appear,' Allegra said. 'Anyway, the press can concentrate on Izzy and Matteo now.' She was appalled that she could be jealous of her own sister—not for the attention, nor for her talent, but because it had been so clear she was singing to someone, that love was in her eyes and voice. That's what burnt. Oh, of course she wanted her sister happy. By the morning she would be okay, but right now, she could not feel lonelier, could not believe the situation she had found herself in, would never have agreed to this if she had known what Alex would be like.

'What happened to you?' She did not care if the driver might be listening, just simply did not care about appearances any more. 'What happened to the man I met in London? The man who came over and spoke to me?'

He could see the palace looming in the night sky and it looked like prison. He could hear her thick voice and knew that tears were falling. He had done this to her—he had trapped her as much as he was trapped himself.

'You've changed.' She hurled the accusation again and he turned his head to face her.

'No.'

'You have!'

'No,' he said it again. 'I have returned to who I am.'

She would never understand him.

'Here I am, Crown Prince Alessandro, here I am on duty at all times. Here there is no time for self, for—'

'Because you make it so,' she insisted. 'Because you and your family lock yourself away in the palace or behind dark glass windows. You're so bloody used to acting the part you've forgotten that you're people too. And your people know it,' she added nastily because, hell, she felt nasty. 'The reason they like me is because I'm real, because I'm *ordinary*.' She hurled the word back at him. 'Because I don't pretend to be perfect, because I don't act as if I'm better than them. No wonder your fans—'

'Fans?' He snorted. 'They are our people, not our fans.'

As they arrived at the palace, before the car had even fully stopped, she jumped out, flew up the steps and into the hall but he was just a step behind her. 'I said the wrong word,' Allegra retorted, 'one wrong word and you jump down my throat, belittle me….' And she did not need to explain herself, did not need a moment more of this.

'What's going on?' His mother came out of the lounge, nursing a brandy, as too often she did these days, her only comfort at night. Alex stood still.

'Nothing.'

'It didn't sound like nothing.'

'She's just upset.' Alex was not about to discuss his love life with his mother! 'She'll be fine in the morning.'

'She'll remember her place, you mean?' Alex blinked at the snarl in his mother's voice. 'Why don't you talk to her?'

'She ran off.'

'Go after her then,' Zoe said, but he just stood there. 'What is it with this family? I thought you were happy, Alessandro. I thought when you brought her home that you wanted a marriage that was worth fighting for.' She gave in then—Zoe, too, did not want to discuss her love life with her son. 'I'm sure she'll be just fine!' she said shrilly, and retreated back to the lounge.

Alex stood—looked up at the stairs—and knew that somehow he had to tell her.

'Leave me alone,' Allegra called as he knocked on the bathroom door. She'd picked up the stupid nightgown that had been laid out on her bed and stormed into the bathroom and even the nightgown enraged her tonight, made her want to spit she was so angry—there were probably hundreds of them, Allegra thought as she undressed. It was probably like a hospital laundry down there, with hundreds of Santina lace nightdresses all whizzing around and around. She hated the mould she was being poured into—had there been scissors in the room she'd have chopped herself a new fringe! She was so angry! As she undressed she almost fell over as she took off her panties then pulled on the beastly gown.

Why, why, why did he have to be like this?

What had happened to the man she had met, the man who had held her, the man who had come so close to making love to her?

Allegra caught sight of herself in the mirror and let out a low moan, because just the thought of that night and his hands on her and her body was leaping with desire, her angry blush burning darker as she recalled the bliss of his touch. All this, *all this*, she could take if she had Alex at night, had the man she loved, the man she craved.

'Allegra.'

She swung around.

Shocked, appalled, embarrassed, because he walked in uninvited. 'What on earth are you doing here?' she hurled.

'We need to talk.'

'I've said everything I'm going to.' She wanted him out of there, hated that she craved him like she never had another. Even angry, even furious, even loathing, she was so turned on she could sink to her knees right now, but furious tears shot out instead.

'I'm going tomorrow.'

'You can't.'

'Just watch me,' she snarled. 'I'm sick of Santina—sick

of living with a family who haven't even got the energy for a decent row, who can sit at the most amazing concert completely unmoved.' She glared at him. 'You can't even *pretend* to love me—you didn't even hold my hand.'

'You don't understand.'

'I don't want to!'

'You have to!' he shouted. 'For tomorrow our wedding date is to be announced.'

'Well un-announce it!' she hissed.

'It's too late for that—you know it. You will marry me….'

'No.' She went to brush past him. 'I'm calling my father.'

'That's another thing…' He blocked the doorway, wondered if she might kick him. But he had to be harsh or he would take her right now in his arms. 'Allegra, you need to remove yourself further from your family.' This he found incredibly difficult. 'You are marrying royalty.' His voice was firm. 'It's not fitting…' He tried to find the words, tried to state out what a royal bride-to-be should already know. Had she been born for this, groomed for this, then it would not need to be said.

'Let me past.' She was furious, completely over this madness. She kicked and she pushed, but he stood firm, held her wrists and told her how it would be.

'If Izzy and Matteo continue, you will see plenty of her.' She knew what he was saying, had known it in her heart, had kidded herself that the lack of contact with her family was just because she was so busy with the wedding and all the things going on in their lives. But in reality she knew that they were being slowly peeled apart and she knew that it must be killing her father, that stepping back to do the supposed right thing must be breaking his heart.

'Let me past.' She was tousled and angry and more

beautiful than he had ever seen her and it would have been so much easier to lie down with her than to stay standing. He could see her breasts rising and falling as she breathed hard in anger, see her erect nipples beneath the lace, her thighs slightly apart in her angry stance and her knickers on the floor. He wanted to kiss his way out of it, to push her from the bathroom to the bed and lose himself in her, to end this row without it ever having to take place. Yet somehow he stood, somehow he had to explain. He let her pass but as she reached for the phone he spoke some more.

'Think before you speak to your father, Allegra—because if it is hell for you, imagine how it might be for Izzy.'

'Izzy?' She swung around, phone in hand.

'From the way your sister was looking to my brother tonight, I think it is no longer just about you.'

She had wanted honesty, wanted to know what went on behind the iron wall that had been around him since they landed here, but now there was dread in her heart, perhaps it already knew, for slowly, like Chinese water torture, the truth was dropping in. 'What does Izzy have to do with us?' She halted then—it felt as if her throat closed over—and he stood and watched as her hellish realisation dawned.

'If I step aside, or if the marriage does not go ahead, Matteo will assume my role. I am quite sure the people of Santina would not be ready for a karaoke queen—though of course she wouldn't be one, there would be no more singing, no more performances....'

'Izzy would never stop.'

'She would have no choice. If the wedding is not announced tomorrow, I will be forced to step aside. It's up to you, Allegra.'

And she tried to picture it, tried to picture Izzy in this role, and as hard as it was for Allegra, it would be hell for Izzy. There was something about Izzy, something fragile, something wild, something precious that would be crushed in a moment by the weight that was landing on Allegra right now. She felt the fight leave her, stabbed at impossible hope.

'Izzy and Matteo might not last....'

'Perhaps not.' Alessandro shrugged. 'But at least it should run its course.' He looked to his fiancée and hated himself for doing this. 'Tomorrow we announce the wedding date. You can, of course, ring your parents first.'

'You won't stop me from seeing them.' She was depleted but still defiant on that point at least.

'Of course you will see them,' Alessandro said. 'It *will* be different though, and more so after the wedding. They can come and see you.' He was most uncomfortable, for though really he couldn't imagine caring if he didn't see his parents for the foreseeable future, he knew that family meant a lot to her.

'It's already different.' She looked to him. 'Have they been spoken to?'

'I would think that the palace would have met with them—would have told them their role in preparing for the wedding.' And then he was honest. 'They spoke with your father, a couple of weeks after the engagement.'

She thought back to that morning on her balcony, to the last *real* conversation she had had with her father, arguing with him about flirting with the queen, and she was hit with a wave of homesickness so violent she thought the boat might topple over.

'What would they have said to him?'

'To pull back, to make sure that all the family does the same. That you were not to be troubled with day-to-day things.'

Like romances and pregnancies and all their gossip. No

wonder she'd felt so out of the loop; her family had been told to keep her out of it for her sake!

'You should have married Anna.' She meant it. 'I wish that you had.'

And he saw her hurt and the mess he had created, his fiancée who was crushed—and the worst part was it had been by his own hand. So his answer was honest, for Allegra's sake:

'I wish I had too.'

CHAPTER TWELVE

She did see her family in the lead up to the wedding, but Alex was right; it wasn't the same.

Izzy was head over heels and naturally assumed Allegra was—she would talk about Matteo for hours, read out songs she'd penned, clump around in her noisy shoes. Because she was Izzy, because she wasn't going to one day be queen, it didn't seem to incense the royals so.

Izzy got to be her wonderful self while Allegra seemed to forget who she was. Two weeks before the wedding Alex had to fly to London to finalise the transfer of his business and would return on the eve of the wedding.

'The eve…!' There had been a row, of course.

Another one.

'There is much business to take care of—when I am back, I will be back for good. We have our honeymoon to look forward to, we are away for a full month,' he pointed out. 'I am just away for two weeks.'

What a difficult two weeks it was, and though she adored spending time with Izzy, it was her fittings with Raymond that got her through—his endless chatter and the smiles he gave her—little shots of confidence that he seemed to inject with every pin he stuck in.

'You've lost more weight.' He was far from impressed. 'Allegra…'

'I'm not trying to.' Allegra stood there and looked at her stick figure and sallow skin and wondered how in a couple of days she was supposed to transform into a radiant bride. She knew she was too thin. Even the queen was offering her croissants these days and she was accepting them too. It was just the nerves and the knot in her stomach and the loneliness that was like an endless furnace on constant high burn. 'Things will calm down after the wedding.' She had to believe that they would, that once they were more alone, once she and Alex were in an apartment, they could form a new normal, that she might find her place in a life she had not chosen.

'Well, let's get this off—it's the last time you'll see it before the big day.'

'Shall I put the other one on?' Allegra asked, but Raymond shook his head. 'You might need to alter it.'

'No need—it's not anywhere near as fitted.' She was curiously disappointed, for she truly loved the other dress. 'Anyway, it's been cleaned and it's hanging.'

'I wanted to see it.'

'You'll see it after the wedding.' Raymond beamed, busying himself with his pins and tapes, trying to hide his blush. For he deliberately hadn't brought it along today; he knew how much better it looked than the other, knew how much more suited it was to Allegra, and he did not want her to know that, did not want her disappointed with her choice of dress on the big day. She had, he knew, enough to contend with already—in truth he was worried about her. 'So,' Raymond asked. 'What have you got planned? Are you off to spend some time with your family?'

'Not till after the rehearsal tomorrow,' Allegra said, trying to pretend it didn't matter. 'Anyway, my dad's got to film his television show and can't get here till the rehearsal.'

'But the rest of them are here,' Raymond said. He was worried about how pale she looked, figured she needed some time with her family. But, in fact, Allegra was petrified to see them in case she ended up breaking down and begging them to just take her home.

'Alex doesn't get in till lunchtime and then I think he's got some royal duties tomorrow night, but I'll be at the hotel, so if I want to see him before the wedding there's only tomorrow afternoon.'

'You'll feel better when you see him,' Raymond soothed. 'You'll remember why you're doing this in the first place,' he said.

She smiled and said she hoped so, but it was the loneliest day of her life when he had gone. She looked out of the window, could see the activity outside the palace, cameras setting up, barriers in place, all getting ready for the day that was fast approaching.

'Allegra.' She answered the phone to Alex. 'How are things?'

'Fine,' she said. 'I've just had my last fitting for my dress. How are things there?'

'I've been busy,' Alex said. 'I am actually looking forward to having a full month off. Is everything sorted?'

'Pretty much,' Allegra said.

'The book?'

'It's almost finished,' Allegra said.

'Really? Well done.' He actually sounded proud. 'Am I allowed to read it?'

'No,' Allegra said. 'I want my father to be the first… Actually…' She stopped herself. 'It doesn't matter.'

'Does it matter or not?' He was always so straight to the point.

'It matters.'

'Well then?'

'I didn't expect to finish so soon, but now that I have I was hoping to give it to Dad at the wedding, to have the book bound—except Santina is not exactly inundated with office shops.'

'You should get it properly bound.'

'It's only a first draft—it isn't even finished.' She couldn't work out the end, didn't want it to be about her wedding, except so much had happened, there were so many changes in her family.

'Email it to me and I will have it bound.'

'You won't read it?'

'Allegra.' He gave a wry laugh. 'I haven't got time to sleep, let alone read.' When Allegra said nothing he concluded the conversation. 'Send it now and I will get Belinda straight on to it. I'll see you tomorrow.'

'Sure.' She hung up the phone, wondered how she could be marrying a man in two days and having such a stilted conversation with him. Maybe he felt the same because almost the moment she hung up, the phone rang again.'

'Alex…?'

'Sorry, only me…' came the lovely sound of Angel. 'We want Allegra!' She heard the cheers in the background. Heard Leo and Ben, Ella and Izzy, all chanting her name. 'Surely you can escape for an extra night.'

'I've got my hair to sort—'

'Allegra…' Izzy came on the phone. She knew better than the rest just how difficult the palace could be at times. 'Just wait there, I'm going to have Matteo send me a car and we're all coming to the palace to get you!'

She fired Alex an email, considered telling him, but chose not to—he would attempt to dissuade her after all. She loved that her siblings had come to rescue her, loved the evening she spent with them, hearing them laugh, catching up on all the news.

Strange that she missed Alex with all this going on.

So much so that the next day, as soon as she awoke, it was Alex she called, even though she knew he would be on his plane.

'He's busy.' It irritated her that Belinda answered Alex's private number.

'Can I speak to him please?'

'He's specifically asked not to be disturbed,' came the snooty response. 'He's having a lie-down.'

And she tried not to think of the bedroom on the private jet that had brought her to here. Tried not to think of Alex and Belinda confined.

It was too hard to.

Especially when tomorrow she would be marrying him.

CHAPTER THIRTEEN

'WHERE is everyone?' Belinda dropped him off and headed straight to the office as Alex walked into a very empty palace on the eve of his wedding.

He'd expected a hive of activity, for Allegra at least to pretend to be pleased to see him, but the welcoming committee consisted of his father at his irritable worst.

'As if anyone would tell me! Your fiancée left yesterday for the hotel to be with her family.'

'I spoke to her yesterday,' Alex said. 'She said she was joining them after the rehearsal.'

'Well, those sisters of hers turned up unannounced, and that ghastly market woman.'

'Chantelle?'

'I really don't need to know her name. Anyway, they've taken her with them.' His son's frown annoyed him. 'You'll see her at the rehearsal.'

Alex knew he'd been cutting it fine, but he'd banked on seeing her, for an hour or two, to check how she was doing. It never entered his head that the cut-off, out-of-control feeling he was experiencing was one he'd subjected his fiancée to these past weeks while in London.

'How is she?'

The king shrugged. 'Permanently premenstrual, I think. She burst into tears the other night because her father can't get here till late this afternoon.' The king let out a smug laugh. 'He's taking part in some celebrity quiz show, in front of a live audience. I think we were supposed to be impressed! Oh—' the king hadn't finished airing his frustrations '—your ex-fiancée is pregnant—baby due in a few months. You certainly backed the wrong horse. We could have had an heir on the way instead of the traveling gypsies descending on Santina.'

'That's all it is to you, isn't it?' Alex looked to his father, actually saw him as if for the very first time. 'You know, I was a little bit worried about my mother's drinking.' He poured himself a rather large one. 'Now I admire her restraint. You'd need to be sedated to listen to you.' But the king wasn't listening.

'Where is she?' the king demanded as the butler served afternoon tea.

And Alex sat there, as an aide spoke about the wedding guests and dignitaries that would be coming. 'You said she was at the hotel.'

'I was talking about your mother. Where is she?' he demanded again. 'We've got the wedding rehearsal this evening, we have guests arriving tonight.'

'She asked for transport,' the butler answered, but was saved from explaining further as the queen arrived home then.

'Where were you?'

'I went into Santina…' She had very pink cheeks. 'I got my hair done, in a salon.' The king just looked at her as if she were speaking a foreign language. 'And Allegra was right, the owner shut up the shop and I had a delightful time with the other women. They were getting their hair done for the wedding too. They're having a street party.' She looked to her king. 'Do you like my hair?'

It was strawberry blonde now rather than grey, but the

king chose not to notice. He didn't want to notice, for he did not like the changes. These trips out were becoming more frequent and he did not like them one bit.

'Have some tea,' he said.

'I'd like a brandy,' she said to a maid. 'And two headache tablets please.'

'It's the crowds,' the king said. 'All the noise giving you a headache.'

'It is not the crowds,' she snapped.

'Have some tea.'

'I don't want tea.'

Alex chose not to listen. Instead he frowned as Belinda came into the room with news he really did not want to hear.

'Bobby Jackson's speaking to the press.'

'You had tea with *him*!' the king said as they moved to the television room. Alex stood at the back, watched Bobby standing at Heathrow Airport, a throng of microphones pressed to his face and a crowd gathered around.

'His people like him,' the queen said.

'They're not his people,' the king snapped, 'they're fans.'

And Alex closed his eyes, for he did not want to be like his father. He knew he could be at times and he never wanted to be like that again—especially where Allegra was concerned. Bobby Jackson was talking about player selection, and giving his views, but now, of course, the questions were growing more personal. The press were bored with incessant 'no comments' and so they chose a different line.

'Will you be making a speech at your daughter's wedding?'

'No comment.' He gave a grim smile and went to walk off.

'Only, you embarrassed her pretty badly at the engagement…'

And Alex watched as Bobby's shoulders stiffened. 'You had a few too many and said how well she'd done for herself.'

And to Bobby's credit he did walk off, but only for two seconds—a proud man, he soon turned around.

'Had I got to finish my speech, I'd have said that Prince Alessandro had done well for himself too. She's a nice girl is Allegra, she's been the lynch pin of this family.' His voice broke just a little. 'They're so lucky to have her. They've done well for themselves too.'

And Alex stood there, and so badly he wanted to see Allegra.

'So vulgar.' The king huffed. 'Off to his harem he goes. I don't know how those women—'

'I'd kill to be Chantelle or Julie.' Just when he least needed it, just when he wanted for the first time to examine his own feelings, there was another crisis to deal with. The queen, his mother, standing with three decades of fury pooling out, as the maid stood there, as the butler did too, as the fireworks went off and the queen exploded. 'At least he gives them half of his attention. I have one man to myself and all I get is ignored. Bobby Jackson is charming, absolutely charming, and yes, rather sexy too. And for all his mistakes, at least he knows how to treat a woman.'

'She'll calm down in moment,' the king said as Zoe marched out of the room. He clicked his fingers to have more tea then changed his mind. 'I might have a brandy.'

And Alex saw the proud old fool and swore he would never be him, and never did he think he would be giving his father marital advice, but then the palace had changed an awful lot since the Jacksons had been allowed in.

There was emotion at every turn, arguments exploding, and Alex realised he would not change it for the world.

'If I were you, Father, I'd ask for two glasses and I'd take the decanter upstairs.'

'She'll be fine in a moment.'

'And maybe,' Alex overrode him, 'you might notice her hair.' He didn't add, Or someone else might. 'And tonight, when the guests have gone and you have retired, I suggest you read this….' He did not feel guilt as he handed over Allegra's work—always efficient Belinda had had two separate copies bound for Allegra to choose from.

'What's this?'

'It's the real story of Bobby Jackson—it shows a man who knows how to forgive. It speaks of love and pride and his devotion to family. How even if others may not approve, he must be doing something right.' He looked to his father. 'After all, look at the children he has raised. But now, I suggest you apologise to your wife—and if you cannot manage that, at least speak with her.'

He watched as after a moment of painful deliberation his father creaked his way out of the chair and nodded to the butler, who handed him the decanter. He looked as if he was walking to the gallows as he climbed up the stairs. Alex never, ever wanted that for Allegra—had never wanted it for Anna either.

That burn in his gut was back. He turned to the butler, then changed his mind; instead he walked into his office and spoke with Belinda.

'I want transport arranged.'

CHAPTER FOURTEEN

'HE SHOULDN'T be much longer.' Belinda clipped off her phone.

'We don't really need Alessandro…' the king said, because he wanted the rehearsal over, was, in fact, rather looking forward to getting back to the palace with his wife! 'He knows his place. Let's just make sure the Jacksons—'

And Allegra bit back a smart retort. She was so sick of the none-too-subtle barbs that the Santinas knew exactly how to do things. Hell, who needed a groom at a wedding rehearsal?

'Where is he?'

Belinda said nothing, but then she had never bothered with Allegra before.

'I'm going to get some air.'

Allegra walked outside, gulping in the cool evening air. She had so badly wanted to see Alex, just for some reassurance. She jumped a little when Belinda walked up beside her.

'They just want to run through the paces one more time. I'll be Alex.'

Allegra could think of nothing worse. 'I'll wait, thanks.'

'The king wants this wrapped up.' Belinda wasn't exactly enamored with Allegra either.

'Then he should call his son.'

'He knows where he is… For goodness' sake, Allegra, do you really need to make a scene? Let's just get on with it.'

'Where is he?'

'Where do you think?'

At that moment a car pulled up—not a royal car, not Alex's car, but a car she did not recognise. She stood in the shadows of the vestry, watching her own heart be served on a plate, watching Alex, the passenger, turn to the driver. There was no mistaking the tenderness in the gesture— watching his hand reach out and cup the driver's face. No mistaking the affection as he leant over and kissed her on the lips and then on her forehead…and they rested their heads there a moment before he pulled away.

'Who?' She hated that it was Belinda she had to ask.

'Anna.' She almost heard the snap of the last string holding her together. 'I thought she was with your brother,' Belinda carried on. 'No doubt he's reassuring her that noth-ing will change.' She could hear the spite in Belinda's voice.

'Did he reassure you the same?' Allegra couldn't help but ask.

Hateful were the eyes that turned to her. 'Do you think for a moment that a wedding ring will stop him? Look around, Allegra. So you get the prince, you get the dress and the pomp, and the title. Enjoy it, enjoy every minute of it, but it won't keep you warm at night.'

'No,' Allegra attempted. 'That's my husband's job!'

But Belinda just laughed; she just stood there and laughed. 'You!' She laughed even louder. 'You really don't get it, do you? The people might think they like you now, but Alex knows it won't last. Just look at you, Allegra, you're nothing. Your family are nothing to him.

And sooner or later they'll be nothing to the people—just a rather embarrassing thorn.'

Allegra stood there, trying to bite back her fury, trying to remember the Allegra of old who could think of a smart retort, the Allegra who was Bobby Jackson's daughter, who would turn around and just give her a black eye.

'The people won't blame him a bit for the way he carries on.' It was unfortunate that at that moment Chantelle chose to wander out of a side door and go through her handbag, coughing a bit, before lighting up a cigarette. 'Now, Anna…' Belinda gave a slightly wistful sigh. 'Anna has class—well, she did, till she met with Jacksons. With Anna, he'd at least have had to show discretion. You lot will take any crumbs.'

'All right, love.' Bobby came over. 'Where is that man of yours?'

'Here I am.' Alex walked over.

'About time.' The king huffed and joined them, as Alex gave Allegra a brief kiss on the cheek, but it was only for show, that much she knew.

'Where were you?'

He frowned down, for never had he had to explain himself before and he certainly wasn't about to start now. Here was hardly the best place to tell his bride of tomorrow that he had spent some time with his ex-fiancée—and certainly not with her in this fragile state. He could see she was shaking, and he didn't like the other changes either: her fringe was long gone now, tucked behind her ear; he could see her clavicles poking out of her chest. He hated what his family had done—what he had allowed.

'I had things to sort out. Come on.' He took her by the elbow and they took their positions at the altar for the rehearsal. He could feel her jangling with nerves. He should never have left her alone to deal with this. He had thought he was doing her a favour, giving her a break before they were forced into the union she didn't want, but instead he'd exposed her.

'What things?' Allegra asked. He heard the sharp *T* at the end of her 'what' and he wanted her back, he wanted Allegra Jackson back.

'At this point, you will join hands...' the priest said.

'What things?' she asked again.

'It is not your concern.'

'It is when you...' And what was the point—what was the point of challenging him? Was this to be her life? To wait in the shadows, to lie in bed and wonder where he was, that he could be so blatant, so dismissive. She loved Izzy, loved her sister so very much, but she loved herself too.

Had to love herself more. She couldn't do this.

'There will be a hymn...' the priest droned on.

'No.' Her voice was soft, so soft that no one noticed, and she said it again.

'No.' The chatter stopped and she looked to her grim fiancé, smelt a perfume that was not hers in the air between them, and her voice was firm when next it came.

'I can't marry you.'

She fled from the church, poured herself into a car and begged the shocked driver to move on.

'Nerves.' Bobby grinned, instantly moving to put everyone at ease.

'It's nerves,' said the king.

'I'm not sure...' Angel had seen the agony on her sister's face as she had fled from the church and she looked to Izzy. 'Shall I go and talk to her?'

'I will,' Bobby said.

'Maybe it will come better from a woman,' Chantelle offered, because the last thing she wanted was Allegra turning this down. She had her outfit sorted and she liked being related to royalty. 'Julie?'

Except Alex had already left the church.

CHAPTER FIFTEEN

'YOU couldn't even last till the wedding!' She opened her hotel door and met him with her rage.

'What are you talking about?'

'I saw you kiss her, saw you hold her....'

'Allegra, you're being ridiculous.'

'I don't want to hear your excuses. You're sleeping with your ex!' Her voice was rising. 'What about Leo, what about my brother? How could you!'

'She's pregnant, for God's sake.'

'I know that.' Allegra sobbed; she was hysterical now, weeks and months of pain, all rising up and there was no horse to jump on to flee away. 'How do I know it isn't yours? You're screwing your ex and—'

He'd heard enough. He grabbed her, his only thought to put an end to her tirade. He could feel anger bubbling up within him, his grip tightening on her, his hand raising to slap her silent and it took every ounce of self-control to lower his hand.

She stared, stunned, appalled, and she waited, breathless, for him to apologise, to recant, but he stood there resolute.

'There would be no self-control if anyone spoke that way of you.'

He meant it.

She knew that and it was not the pain of his hand on her arm but the strange honor in his words that brought tears to her eyes.

'Anna and I have never slept together—she kept herself for me. As future queen this was to be her expected gift. Of course things have changed,' he hurriedly added. 'I have had harsh words with my father that you are never to be questioned, that your past is your own....'

She closed her eyes in shame, because even if it felt things moved at a snail's pace, he had ensured changes, had moved impossible mountains, even if she had not known.

'I went to see Anna because I wanted to speak with her and it seemed imperative I do that before the wedding. For so long there had been guilt. I never intended to hurt her with our engagement, never intended that she find out the way she did, through the press. Ours was supposed to be a brief fling, and now she has had to come attend our wedding. I needed to put things right with her. She's happier than she ever has been. She sees it was the best thing that could happen. Anna and I could never have divorced.'

'Unlike us.'

And she could never read him, could spend the rest of her life trying to work him and still not get him, for even as she stood, he surprised her again.

'I don't want a divorce, Allegra.' He said it as if he meant it. 'I am going to do everything that I can to make this marriage work. There was no attraction with Anna—I care for her,' he admitted, 'but...' How could he say it? 'It would have been my parents' marriage all over again— perfunctory sex to produce an heir.'

'You couldn't put *her* through it, yet you will me.'

'There would be nothing perfunctory about us.'

'A loveless marriage, but with good sex?'

'I can think of worse things.'

'What about Belinda?' Her eyes were savage again. 'She said—'

'Never listen to a scorned woman—you know that. Belinda is bitter. I have not slept with her since you and I met. As of tomorrow, she no longer works for me. I have ensured her position in my old company, or a package if she prefers, but—'

'She wants you.'

He nodded.

'She can't have me though. I will be adhering to my vows. It's up to you if you marry me, Allegra. I am not going to beg. I'm certainly not going to grovel. The choice is yours, but when tonight you make your decision, there is one thing you ought to know. I have no intention of staying celibate, and as I have just told you, no intention of sleeping around—which means you and I will sleep together,' Alex said. 'If you marry me tomorrow we will share a bed.'

'And if I don't?'

'Then don't turn up. I love my brother, but I am not living like a monk for his sake. You know that whatever there is not between us, that much there is….'

'You're so sure.'

Tender now were the fingers that moved along her arm, yet she flinched. He roamed a hand down her body and she curled inside. Then he moved a hand to her cheek and she turned it away, but cool were his lips on her flesh and she closed her eyes, berating the bliss his mouth delivered.

'I hate what you do to me.'

'You won't tomorrow,' Alex said. 'If you come to the church, then know that you will be my wife in every sense of the word. It's up to you. Know that I will be a good husband, a wonderful provider, that your family will be taken care of and you will be too.'

'You need to know something too. The people of Santina have been unhappy for a long time.'

'I do not need your opinion on my people.'

'You can dismiss what I say if you want, but you will do me the courtesy of at least listening. The people want me, because I am ordinary, because I cry and I laugh, even in public, because of—not in spite of—my family's mistakes. You marry *me*, or you can find another wife to wear the nightdresses laid out for her, perhaps one with quieter shoes, and she can be as miserable as your mother is.'

'Don't…'

'Don't what?' Allegra said. 'Don't speak of such things? Why not?' Allegra demanded. 'Why can't you have an honest conversation with the woman who tomorrow might be your wife? And know this too—my family will come and visit me in the palace and I shall fly home and visit them. I will be close with my brothers and sisters. If you want to marry me, know who you're committing to.'

'I do,' Alessandro said, and he surprised her with a smile, the smile he gave her on the first day, the smile that always melted her so. And then he did the impossible, at least the impossible for a prince in Santina—he made a joke. 'I'm just getting in practice for tomorrow. I do, Allegra.'

CHAPTER SIXTEEN

'How is she?' Matteo, Ash and Hassan were waiting when he returned to the palace.

'She's okay,' Alex said.

'Bobby asked if you could ring him and let him know,' Matteo said, and Alex nodded. 'He wants to have a word with you.'

'There's no need.' The king huffed. 'He's probably there now—he can see her for himself.'

Alex ignored him. 'I need his number.'

'Don't you have it?' Zoe asked. 'Didn't you ring him first when you went to ask for his daughter's hand? What about when you were in London?'

There were so many things he had done wrong, so many, many things. As Matteo gave him the necessary number Alex moved into the library to talk with his soon-to-be father-in-law in private, closing his eyes in shame as he spoke to him.

'Right,' the king said as Alessandro came out. 'Let's have a drink—we'll have guests arriving shortly.' They did, dignitaries that had to be entertained on the eve of the wedding, essential duty to be taken care of, but Alex halted the procession making their way to the drawing room.

'Actually there's been a change of plan. I'm going out with Bobby tonight.' He saw Matteo smother a smile, saw

Hassan raise an eyebrow. 'And with Allegra's brothers, my friends too.' He nodded to Ash, who had married his sister, and Hassan, who had married Allegra's sister. 'With family.'

'Out?'

'It's tradition.'

'For the Jacksons perhaps…'

'I'm marrying a Jackson, in case you hadn't noticed.' He glanced to his brother and friends. 'Come on.'

CHAPTER SEVENTEEN

She awoke surprisingly calm, and smiled at the room service attendant who brought her coffee. She then sat up in bed and flicked the remote to turn the television on, finding it hard to believe that the chatter and excitement and the images playing out on the television screen were for *her* wedding.

The streets were filling already, the people of Santina eager to get the best viewpoint of the guests making their way to the church, and though logic told her that she should be nervous, sad even, Allegra was not. She refused to be the martyr bride.

She was marrying the man she loved today.

And that was something to celebrate.

She sat, eyes closed, as her make-up was done and the final touches were put to her hair, but opened them when the door knocked. In came her bridesmaids—Angel and Izzy looking stunning, and two little cousin princesses from Alex's side.

'Your dad's got the most terrible hangover.' Angel laughed as she twirled in her bridesmaid's dress. 'I don't think your groom will be feeling much better. From all reports it was quite a heavy night.'

'Alex?' Allegra frowned. 'He was at the palace last night....'

'How little she knows!' Angel rolled her eyes. 'Your fiancé, Matteo and Hassan were out with Bobby and Co.'

'They came here to the hotel?'

'No.' Angel grinned. 'They went into town. Apparently the locals were thrilled, plying the wedding party with sambuca.'

Allegra let out a gurgle of laughter. She was quite sure Angel must have got it wrong somehow; perhaps Alex had dropped in to be polite or they had somehow run into one another. But it was nice to laugh this morning, especially when there was a knock at the door and Raymond came in with his entourage wheeling the much-coveted dress that was covered in layers of sheets.

'You're looking better.' Raymond beamed.

'I feel better,' Allegra admitted.

'Can I see?' Izzy asked.

'No, you cannot!' Raymond scolded. 'I am not risking a single eyelash falling onto this dress. I want everyone out—you can see her when she's dressed.' And he shooed out the bridesmaids and pulled off a sheet and there it was—full skirt, in at the waist and with a very long train. It glimmered and was absolutely beautiful. The thing was, it simply wasn't the one that she loved.

'I'm wearing the other one, Raymond.'

'Oh, Allegra.' His eyes widened. 'The queen…'

'What's she going to do?' Allegra asked. 'Turn me away at the church?' She saw the excited grin on her designer's face. 'He's marrying me, Raymond. The "me" he first met…' And Raymond understood, for he had got back together with Fernando but had decided to end things.

'You're wonderful,' Raymond said.

'So are you!' She gave him a hug and then Raymond danced off.

'It's so much better!' Raymond admitted, pulling off the sheet. 'So, so much more you.'

It was. It was stunning, so beautiful she could hardly breathe. But before she took off her robe, before she slipped it on, she turned to the hairdresser who was pulling out her veil from a large box.

'I know it's terribly short notice,' Allegra said. 'And I know it's not what we planned, but is there any chance you could cut me a fringe?'

It was nice to find her power, wonderful, at the eleventh hour, to find her voice, to see the real Allegra returning as she stood in the most beautiful dress in the world. She looked into the mirror and smiled at the bride she was and the princess she would become.

She would be a wonderful wife; she would be loyal to her husband and she would readily give the love that inside burnt, but she would be her own person too.

Would have coffee with her sisters and nights out too, would not walk away from her family—no matter what.

'Last-minute change!' A boot-faced florist walked in, cursing in rapid Italian as she added some blue-starred flowers to the heavy white rose bouquet. *'Erbacce...'* the florist sneered. Allegra knew from her lessons that that meant 'weeds,' but they were her favourite weeds in the world. And perhaps, even with the meticulous planning, they had forgotten something blue after all!

'Oh, Allegra.' She looked to her father and he took out a hanky and blew his nose. 'You look amazing.' And then, in that moment before they walked to where the cars were waiting, Bobby had to make sure.

'You do want this?'

She nodded, but she couldn't speak. Tears were terribly close, but despite it all, it was what she wanted.

'It's not too late, you know...' Bobby checked.

'I love him, Dad.'

Bobby rolled his eyes and then conceded. 'I know you do. And yep, I thought he was a cold fish, but he went up in my books last night.' So they had been out! Allegra wasn't too sure that she needed the details, but she did smile at the very thought. 'I just want to make sure you're happy. That you know what you're getting into.'

She knew.

'I always moaned to your mum and Chantelle that you and your sisters' weddings would bankrupt me.' It broke her heart how hard it must be for him. 'This should be a dream come true for a parent, hasn't cost me a penny, and what with Izzy and Matteo, Ella and Hassan, Angel and Rafe…' He faltered for a moment. 'Careful what you wish for, huh!'

'You're not giving me away today, Dad.'

He frowned. 'Another thing they're taking away from me?'

'I meant…' Her voice was very firm, very clear, and her eyes shone, not with tears, but with absolute faith in her words. 'I'm always going to be your daughter—I'm not going to let them change that part of me. We'll still see each other, you'll come here and I'm not missing out on Christmas.' She saw an edge of a smile. 'And I mean that. And if Alex doesn't want to join in, if duty means he can't, I'm going to be there. Maybe just for one night, maybe we'll have to do Christmas some years on Boxing Day, but I'm not missing it—and neither will Izzy, I'll make sure of that. You're not giving me away, Dad.'

'No, I'm gaining a cold fish!'

He always made her laugh.

'Let's do it then.'

CHAPTER EIGHTEEN

'You don't have a cigarette?' He saw Matteo frown. 'Joking,' Alex said, but there was this restlessness in him, this gnaw, as they waited for the car that would take him to the church.

'Worried she might not show up?' his brother teased.

'No,' Alex said, for it was not that which worried him. There was this uneasiness that was ever present these days, this churn in his stomach that had him swallow an antacid and wait for the burn to go—it did not.

'What are you doing?' Alex asked, irritated as his brother tapped on his phone.

'Just checking on Izzy,' Matteo said. 'She'll be nervous about singing at your reception tonight.' He glanced up. 'Sorry. I'm supposed to be taking care of the groom. Mind you, you're hardly the type for nerves.'

'Ask Izzy how Allegra is,' Alex said.

'I was joking about her not showing up.' Matteo grinned, but it was not that that concerned Alex as his brother awaited Izzy's response. It was something else, something he could not place.

'Izzy's already said goodbye to Allegra, she says...' Matteo did not continue, instead he grinned at whatever Izzy had said.

'She makes you happy?' Alex asked.

'You know she does.'

'I don't know,' Alex said, and for a second there it felt as if Matteo were the older one, the wiser one, privy to something he had never seen. 'You love her?'

'I do,' Matteo said, not at all shocked by his brother's question, because in this family love did not rule.

'How did you know?'

'Apart from the fact she was the first woman to swim in my fountain?' He gave a ghost of a smile. 'I'd never met anyone like Izzy before. The woman drove me crazy. And yes, it took me a while to realise that "crazy" was actually love.' He looked at his older brother. 'I nearly lost her, Alex. Don't make the same mistake as me.'

'I'm marrying her today,' Alex pointed out.

'I thought we were talking about love,' Matteo said. 'Which in this family is another subject entirely. Come on,' Matteo continued. 'Can't have the groom being late.'

Alex made a phone call, just a quick one, heard the confusion at the other end, but chose not to justify.

'You will see that it is done,' Alex said then clicked off his phone and climbed in the vehicle, stared unseeing out of the car window as they drove to church. He tried not to think of her smile and the feel of her in bed beside him and her raw tears last night. Tried not to think of the life he had trapped her in, a life she did not want, a loveless marriage that served only the people.

The streets were lined with people all waving and cheering, but they did not expect him to wave, nor even smile, for Alessandro so rarely did, but he did look—he looked at the hopeful faces, saw the pictures they held up of Allegra. They were his people, and reluctant or not, a little too soon for his liking perhaps, now he took his role on, and as he did in everything he would perform to perfection.

He and his bride *would* bring fresh ways to Santina.

The wait was interminable, and despite brave words to his brother, he did wonder if she'd change her mind, if at the last minute she would leave him standing. But then he heard the shift in the music, the excited chatter build in the church behind him, and then a shuffle as the congregation rose. He did not turn around; instead he stared ahead and the moment he had dreaded for the whole of his life was here. Except as he heard the congregation hush, the gnaw in his gut that should have tightened seemed to fade, the ache and the void seemed to fill....

He remembered the day he had met her; the loneliness that had twisted him as he'd sat in the club had been replaced by the first honest conversation he had ever had—how an afternoon with her had made the world seem right.

And he closed his eyes for he could not fathom it.

Then he opened them again, and the thought was the same.

At eight minutes past two as she started to walk towards him, Alex fell in love with his bride.

Had loved her all along, Alex realised as he turned around to see her, spent his days trying not to think of her, trying not to admit what he had thought impossible for him.

And he expected pain in her face and for her to be shaking and full of nerves—except she was smiling, a little pale, holding Bobby's arm tightly as she walked towards him, but she was walking with eyes wide open and her head held high.

His mind was playing a trick on him.

Aware of the cameras on him, aware at a wedding like this there could be no surprises, that till the formalities ended late into the night this was duty, he was, as always, supremely composed as he faced her.

And every camera that was trained for a reaction saw

his slow smile, saw him look away and then back again.
He continued to stare, a dust of colour on his neck spread-
ing to his ears, for surely every one could see—for, if he
squinted a little, if he left her just a little out of focus, it
could almost be their engagement night. She could almost be walking towards him in her nightgown, for the
lace draped her body, seeped into chiffon on her arms and
around midthigh, the chiffon seeming to fade on her legs
and arms. It was Santina lace, and a secret smile played on
her face as his thoroughly modern bride walked towards
him. Allegra was back and his heart twisted with love
and pride as she joined him and peered up at him from
beneath her fringe.

'Allegra...' He could feel the cameras on him. He
wanted to say it here, but the priest was already talking,
the first hymn being sung and time was galloping along.
It killed that she'd marry him without knowing that he
loved her.

It did not kill her to stand there.

She stared at her groom and said her words clearly.

She would love him till death, she said, for it was true,
even if sooner they must part.

Then she looked down, not shy but just deep inside
herself, because she could not look him in the eyes as he
lied—and did he have to say his vows so clearly, did he
have to not waver, to sound so convincing? She felt his
hand tighten and she looked up, saw those liquid brown
eyes and their intensity; he was a fine actor, for she was
the only one in the room who knew the truth.

There was no moment to talk, for each one had been
meticulously taken care of. There were photos on the steps
of the church and one tiny unscheduled moment when
Allegra stepped towards the crowd, throwing her bouquet
into the people, returning the flowers that they had given

her—the little blooms that she'd carried home after her jaunts into the town, the little petals that had brightened so many lonely days.

Then they were whisked away to the palace, formal photos where the Jacksons stood with wide smiles and the Santinas just a touch more reserved, perhaps in nervous anticipation of the party tonight!

The photographer was respectful but this was his moment and he was damned if he didn't get the perfect shot. But the king was distracted, his wife beaming by his side, and then later at the bridal breakfast, utterly and completely radiant, he'd heard her laughing, a laugh that was unfamiliar, a laugh that maybe he'd missed.

It was hell for Alex, standing there, holding her, smiling with her, knowing she was lonely, knowing the truth he had to share.

They were in the horse carriage, heading back to the palace.

'Just rest for a couple of hours,' the aide informed them, because, well, they needed to and everyone knew that the wedding was just a formality. They'd been sharing a bed for ages after all. 'We'll be back to do your hair and make-up at five—you'll make your entrance at six-thirty.'

And finally they were alone.

'You look amazing,' Alex said.

'It's actually incredibly uncomfortable,' Allegra admitted. She smiled at the maid who came in to help her undress, for she would be expected to wear the gown tonight, but for now it would be a relief to take it off.

'We'll manage, thanks.' It was Alex who dismissed the maid and she was suddenly nervous, knew, despite her confidence in her decisions, that she was now his bride and that all the bravado in the world could not tame her shyness.

'Let me help,' Alex insisted as she stood there impossibly shy, far braver in her role of princess than wife.

He was behind her and his fingers undid the tiny buttons.

'Really, there is nothing very romantic about wedding attire.' She gave a brittle smile as she eyed his military uniform. 'Maybe we should call back the maid...' She was blabbering and terribly so.

'We'll manage,' Alex said, which meant rather than drop his braided jacket to the floor he placed it on a chaise longue and then sat on it and took off long boots. Her heart was in her mouth as she slipped her dress off and stepped out of it.

'I need to hang it.' God, the one time she needed the maid... Instead she was dressed in a stupid basque with hands that were shaking so, for she could feel his eyes now roam her body, could hear the undoing of zips and buckles and guessed he was close to naked now. And somehow she had to hang the most talked-about dress in the country.

'Come to bed, Allegra.'

'I can't sleep with you now.' Determined to be honest, determined to be true to herself, she said it without looking at him. Instead she arranged the chiffon so that it would hang nicely this evening. 'I mean, I know that's probably what's expected, and I know that we will, but—'

'Allegra...'

'I'm just nervous enough about tonight, about the speeches, about my family, about so many things, without...' She padded to the ensuite and slipped off her bridal underwear and slipped on a robe, and chatted nervously away. 'I'm just so tired and so wound up and...' She tried to be honest. 'I don't want to be rushed.' She walked back to the room, glad he had turned off the light, glad for the thick drapes that shut out the late-afternoon light, glad for a couple of hours to regroup. 'And no doubt we will later, but it's hard to explain. I mean, it must be a walk in the park for you....'

'A walk in the park?'

His English was excellent, just there were certain things that didn't translate, and she actually smiled as, still dressed in her robe, she climbed into bed beside him. 'No big deal.'

It was a huge deal, except to tell her that would sound pushy. 'When you're ready.'

He heard her sigh of relief.

'Can I just sleep?' She wriggled at the very pleasure of it. 'I didn't sleep much last night.'

'I know.'

He stared up into the darkness and he waited, for the rush of thoughts, for thirst, for the burn in his gut, and instead he breathed in air that smelt of her and all there was was peace.

'I had Matteo ask after you when he texted Izzy this morning.'

'Mmmm.'

'She was already heading for the cars though.'

Allegra closed her eyes. It was such a minor detail in the scheme of things, but rare for Alex to be the one filling silence, talking about nothing. 'I was worried.'

'That I wouldn't show up?'

'No,' Alex said. 'Though I thought you might not.' He turned and looked at her half dozing. 'You seem...' He did not know how to best describe it. 'I thought you would be more...'

'Miserable.' She peeked open an eye. 'No.'

'How come?' Alex asked, because she was a different woman to yesterday.

'I realised I was marrying the man I love.'

He felt the heat from her body, not passion, but a blush, because it was a brave thing indeed to admit, when you knew it was not reciprocated. He lay there with his breath held in his lungs and he frowned because her eyes were closed and she was half asleep.

'What does it feel like?' he asked.

'Painful,' Allegra said. 'But you learn to live with it.' She rolled over, she really would sleep. She'd told him—it would hardly make the news; after all, everyone thought that she did.

'You love me?'

'Why else would I be in your bed, Alex? Believe me, I'm not here for the million pounds, and as much as I love her, I'm not here for Izzy. My freedom's worth a lot more to me.'

'When?' he asked. 'Since when?'

'I'm not sure…' she mused in the darkness. 'Probably when I excused myself to go the ladies'….'

'The first day we met?' he asked, but he was not waiting for an answer from Allegra. Instead he was questioning himself, for it was that day that he had for the first time truly spoken to another. Not even his brother nor his be-trothed had heard his darkest thoughts, yet he had shared them easily with Allegra.

'Tell me this pain.'

'I can't.' She was tired, so tired. Her feet ached, her head pulsed with the sound of cheers and bells and she was lying next to the most beautiful man on God's earth. But if san-ity was to be her savior, if she didn't want to fall asleep at her own wedding party, then she really needed to sleep.

'Is it like wanting chocolate?'

'Dunno.'

'Then you eat and that is not what you want.'

'Maybe.'

'Where nothing tastes right?'

'A bit.'

'When you think it is sex you want, but you know it's not what you need.'

'Do we have to talk about…?' She didn't want Belinda in the room with them, didn't want to hear about his failed attempts to screw his way out of this.

'When you can't look at another woman,' Alex continued. And maybe she did want to hear after all. 'Because even though that always worked before, now you find that all you want is her?' He continued and her mind was dizzy. 'Where you ask your brother to text because you want to know, not what she is doing, but that she is okay?'

And she opened her eyes to him.

'Where you kick yourself over and over, where you lie awake at night and berate your choice of a single word, because when you said "ordinary—"' he heard her sob, felt her burn in shame and he hated himself for ever saying it '—that you meant she was normal, that this was not the life for her, and you hate yourself for saying it?'

'Why didn't you tell me?'

'I didn't know.' He lay there bemused by his own revelation. 'Never, not for a minute, did I consider I might love my bride.' He turned to her. 'It was not a factor.…'

'Like describing a rainbow to a blind man.' She saw him frown and she smiled. 'It's a saying. Like, how can you describe something you've never seen, something the other has no comprehension of.'

He looked to his past, to his rich, privileged life, and now that love lay next to him, now that love lived inside him, he understood her words. 'For all that my parents said about your family, for all I have said,' he stepped up, 'there is so much love there. And I do,' he said. 'I do love you.'

'When…' It was her turn.

'At about eight minutes past two,' he admitted. 'When I said my vows I meant them.'

And he kissed her because he couldn't not. A kiss that was different to any Alex had ever delivered, for kisses had always been precursors, just not today. He kissed her and he tasted her and he loved her with his mouth. And because he loved her with his mind, because there was for ever ahead of them, because he wanted this to be right, he pulled away.

'Sleep.'

'How can I possibly sleep now?'

'You're tired,' he said

'Not now.'

'Allegra.' It was Alex who wriggled away, because he was impossibly hard with her next to him, wanted her so badly, but was determined and weighted with responsibility, for an hour had passed and they had at best an hour or more. It had been so far from perfect for her, by his hand, by his cruel mouth, that he wanted at least to get this right.

'Rest now,' he said, 'and then tonight…' He could hardly wait, but for her he would. 'I want to do you properly later.' And sometimes his brain moved faster in his native tongue than his mouth allowed for translation, but if it was crass and not quite what he meant, from her peal of laughter he had not offended.

'You're going to *do* me properly, are you?'

'Yes.' He grinned. 'Now rest. Or…' He couldn't wait to tell her. 'I was going to give you this tonight.' He reached over to the bedside table.

'I don't need a gift…' She didn't, especially when he went to the dresser drawer and pulled out a velvet box. She loved him and everything, and was completely, incredulously delighted that he loved her too, but she'd received so many jewels today. Really, the one she loved

most and would love the most for ever was the emerald
he had bought on the day they had met.

Still, she knew she had nothing to complain about, so
she smiled as she took the box and was ready to say a big
wow in surprise as she undid the clip, but instead, as she
opened the box, she frowned.

'Keys?'

'They are the thing I miss most when I am here. Even
the car is brought around, but as soon as I get to London...'
She smiled as she looked at the simple silver key ring
holding two keys. Yes, Alex was right, she had not used a
key in all the time she'd been in Santina. 'I wanted somewhere for you as I know how much you need your family.
I wanted you to have somewhere, a place that was yours
when you visit, a place they can go if you choose....' She
looked at the man who must have loved her even when
he didn't know it because it was the most thoughtful
gift in the world. 'A home in London—maybe you can
host Christmas one year.' She laughed through her tears,
laughed that he knew how important her family was, and
she could feel all the love and hope for their future wrapping around her as did his arms. 'There's a car too,' he said.
'I have to arrange for it to be driven each week, so that the
battery doesn't go flat.' She loved his constantly working
brain, and he loved that she didn't even care what make
the car was and they loved that they finally had each other.

'Oh, Alex...' She didn't know what to say. 'I—'

'Don't!' he interrupted. 'I did not expect a gift. I don't
want you to be embarrassed.'

'I'm not,' she said, and she wasn't. 'And I do.'

'What.'

'I'm not embarrassed and I do have a gift. A gift I can
only give one other.' And she leant over and gave him a
kiss, and then whispered into his ear. She moved back so

she could watch it sink in as he found out that his modern bride was, in fact, rather old-fashioned after all.

'Tonight,' he said, overcome with the enormity, pale at the thought of how her first time might have been, for that morning in bed he would not have been gentle. 'Tonight, we will take our time....'

But she could not wait now for tonight, because love unleashed her.

Not her love but his.

His love made her brave and she'd waited so very long, and even a few hours' delay was an impossible task.

As he lay and tried to pretend that he was dozing, as he tried to force his breathing to at least sound deep and even, wondered if he should throw in a snore for good measure, he felt the soft roll of her into him, and the hand that swept along his chest and touched him. He tried very hard to keep breathing as her hand crept down.

She felt the flat firm plane of his chest, the flat smooth areola and the tautness of nipples that had never been beneath her fingers, and she toyed there for a moment, because she could.

Because he was hers and for exploring and she was more curious than shy.

He smelt so clean—he always had, this tangy citrus scent that only belonged to him, her private perfumery. She breathed in the scent she would crave for ever, the private scent of cologne and this man, the undressed aroma that teased in her nostrils and demanded a taste and a kiss on his chest.

And he could not pretend to be sleeping, as he held his breath as her hand slid down to his hardness, his moan confirmed what she knew and no, he could not wait.

He rolled on to her, took her mouth with his and kissed her as he never had, nor never would another. His hands roamed her body, the body that had roamed his mind and that led him to the sweet warm place that had been re-served for him, finding her smooth and oiled, tenderly he stroked her, his fingers moving in to gently stretch but Allegra did not want that.

'You,' she said. 'I want you.' And so badly he wanted her, too, that in answer his legs nudged her thighs apart.

'I won't hurt you,' he said. 'I'll be slow.'

'No,' she said. 'Don't hold back.' He was holding her, his face in her hair, her hands on his back, and she didn't want slow and tender; she wanted the passion and pain that came with love. 'We only get this moment once.'

And this moment was theirs and they shared it. He pressed into her and she accepted; he pierced her and he made her a lover and he captured her heart. It hurt and it was delicious, a unique hurt that he made that bonded her to him. And as she grew accustomed to the feel of him inside her, as she shivered with each measured stroke, she felt him try not to hasten, but her body accepted him now, moved with him now and willed him on to abandon.

'Am I hurting you?'

'No.' She wanted every piece of him, wanted him rough and desperate for she was desperate with new sensations and so too was Alex. An emotional virgin; he lost it, too, that afternoon, because he went to a place where he had never been. He shared his heart and told her he loved her as he came; she wanted to stay in bed with him forever, did not want to dress, wanted to stay behind closed doors.

The phone shrilled by the bed—duty calling loudly, for no servant would dare enter on their wedding day.

'Leave it,' Alex said.

'We'll be late for our own wedding party.'

They would be, by the time they had bathed and hair and make-up was redone, Allegra was back in her wedding gown, Alex in his uniform. They were running a full thirty minutes behind schedule!

'Your father will be having a fit.'

'No.' Alex frowned into his phone as he took a message from Matteo. 'It would seem that my parents are running late too.'

And then he told her.

'I read your book.' He smiled and she blushed. 'I gave it to my father to read too.'

'Alex!'

'I admire your father.'

'Thank you,' Allegra said, because it meant an awful lot to hear, and then she laughed. 'Well, it's lovely of you to say that, but I hope you don't admire him for certain things. I want a very different husband….'

'You've got one,' Alex said, and she didn't just believe him, she knew in her heart it was true. 'But I have learnt from him and I hope my father does too. I will be a better father for reading your words, a better husband and a better prince.' He took her arm and asked if she was ready.

'Are you!' Allegra asked. 'The last party…' She still blushed at the memory, as lovely as they were, her family truly could be shocking.

'I'm looking forward to this one,' Alex admitted; in fact, they both were.

It wasn't out with the old; it was a welcome into the new.

He kissed his new bride and he told her.

'I'm looking forward to life with you.'

EPILOGUE

'ONE more!' The photographer was annoyingly insistent, and as she stood for *one more* shot before she headed into the evening party, Allegra actually wanted to see the photo in the morning, for surely she somehow looked different, surely it would be obvious to the world what had just occurred—that the happy couple had just fallen in love? That her body still thrummed from his touch.

But the photographer wanted his final formal shot; for tonight, there were no cameras allowed. As the royal newlyweds entered and the doors closed behind them, there was a feeling of relief. The day had gone brilliantly, the night…well, who knew, but tonight old money and new would mingle.

'You look stunning.' Bobby beamed as she stepped in and accepted a glass of champagne. 'Oh, and I didn't get a chance to say it earlier. Zoe…' He turned to the queen. 'You look amazing. Love the hair!'

Alex said nothing, at least not till they were safely on the dance floor. In public, even on his wedding night, he was still on duty, still the cold fish her father assumed, but as they danced there were words between them, words no one else heard. The love between them was palpable.

Because as Izzy started to sing, as the senior couples started to dance, everyone saw that she laughed as Alex said something to his bride, something that made her throw her head back and laugh.

'He is flirting.'

'He's not.' Allegra laughed. 'He's just...Dad.'

'My poor father.' Alex groaned, watching Eduardo hold his wife just a little tighter.

'He's never been happier.' Allegra smiled and then rested her head on his shoulder, could hear Izzy's glorious voice filling the room. Even if she had wanted to stay in bed, she could now happily stay in this moment forever, dancing with her husband, her family and his together and love filling the room.

'Soon we do speeches.' He held her a bit tighter. 'You could give your father the book then.'

'Can you?' Allegra asked. 'As part of your speech?'

'I would be proud to.'

'After that, you throw your bouquet...' He stopped. 'That's right, you don't have one.'

'I'm sorry,' Allegra said. 'It just seemed the right thing to do.'

'It was the right thing to do,' Alex said. 'The people deserve to be a part of today.' He gave her a smile, that smile, the one that would forever win her heart. 'Did you like the flowers I had added?'

'You!' Allegra said. 'I thought it was because we'd forgotten blue.'

'Blue?' Alex frowned, because he had never heard of that tradition. 'Always the bride carries white roses, picked from the Santina palace—it seemed wrong. When I drive through Santina now, as my plane comes into land, when I see those flowers dotted everywhere, always it makes me think of you.'

'Your common weed,' Allegra teased.

'No—I am having it renamed. It will be our national

flower, the Santina Star. I have realised that to us it is ordinary, but to the world it is extraordinary.' He kissed her cheek; he pulled her in a little closer and she blossomed inside, her heart unfurling that last little bit as his mouth found her ear.

'Just as you are to me.'

* * * * *

Congratulations to Alex & Allegra,
Their Majesties the Crown Prince and Princess
of Santina!

Read on for an exclusive peek
behind the palace walls for an update
on the rest of the Santina Royal Family!

Dearest Sophia

How lovely it was to see you and Ash and the twins over Christmas, and thank you so much for the gorgeous ruby earrings—so like you to remember that rubies are my favourite stone.

It was wonderful to see you and Ash so obviously happy together. He's a changed man, Sophia, or rather he has become the truly charming and delightful man he promised to be in his youth. When I said as much to him he told me that that is all down to you and your love for him. Indeed I could hardly get him to stop praising you and the boys or to talk about anything or anyone else. To see him behaving so lovingly and tenderly towards you and the boys was a delight. He quite adores you. The love between you both is so plain to see and so strong. As a mother I could not ask for more for you.

Ash was full of praise for the work you are doing with his people, and that of course made your father feel very proud. Just to see the two of you with your twin sons so obviously happy together truly lifted my heart. Your father and I are looking forward so much to our coming royal visit to you.

Sophia, I am so pleased that you have found the happiness you deserve.
Your loving mother,
Zoe

Jackson Nets Mega Book Deal
(Exclusive to *PWOAR!* magazine!)

Bad-boy ex-soccer star Bobby Jackson has scored again—but this time not with one of the many love-lies who graced the legendary sportsman's bed. Jackson has just signed an exclusive two-book deal with publisher Spills & Moon, in what promises to be a rip-roaring tell-all story about his exploits, both on *and* off the pitch.

For those too young to remember the tousle-haired centre-forward whose prolific goal-scoring thrilled schoolboys and teenage girls alike, Jackson latterly became more famous for his chequered love life, than for his ball skills.

After fathering six children (by three different women!) and making and losing several fortunes in the process, Jackson is no stranger to publicity. But fans and enemies are keen to know whether he will throw some light on the persistent claim that his father was a distant relative of the present prime minister.

Jackson is currently holidaying in Kashamak, where his daughter Ella is now queen, and could not be reached. From a Bedouin tent just outside the main city of Samaltyn, where *PWOAR!* caught up with her, the new queen gave an enigmatic smile when asked for her reaction to the book.

Her husband, Sheikh Hassan, was not available for comment.

BEN & NATALIA...

From *Up Close!* magazine:

Last night high-powered celebrity couple Ben and Natalia Jackson attended a gala event to benefit several charities that support services for those with dyslexia and other learning disabilities. Natalia, the daughter of the king of the island principality Santina, spoke movingly about her own battle with dyslexia and the support she is now receiving as an adult. Her husband, Ben, entrepreneur and son of ex-footballer Bobby Jackson, looked on proudly before claiming his new bride in a dance. Natalia looked stunning in a halter-neck gown in silver satin with matching wrap. The happy couple posed for an exclusive photograph with *Up Close!* and all proceeds will go to several charities of their choice. The Jacksons recently honeymooned in Rome, and they intend to divide their time between London and Santina. When asked, Natalia replied with a twinkle in her eye that her children would need to spend at least half the year on her native island. Could baby bliss be in the Jacksons' near future?

RAFE & ANGEL...

Email from Angel McFarland, Lady Pembroke, to Princess Allegra:

Here's something that will make your blood run cold: I've somehow turned into a nature lover after all this time in the wilds of Scotland. The horror! I've become obsessed with the gardens, to the deep dismay of the poor gardener, who is forced to contend with me. I have personally planted whole beds of flowers and even a shrub or two, and I have opinions about the state of the woods. Can sheep herding be far behind?

Lest you become too worried and consider sending off a royal search party to find me and restore me to my former glory, I haven't completely let myself go. (Of course not! I am nothing if not vain up here in the middle of nowhere.) I do pride myself on wearing totally inappropriate couture while tramping about the grounds. I know, I know. Today's charmingly offbeat countess will become tomorrow's village lunatic, my eccentricities whispered about behind every local hand. There are worse fates.

We've opened the manor house to the public for the first time this spring, and I'm having a wonderful time playing docent to all the tourists. (And there are so many! Who knew that people actually come to the Scottish Highlands deliberately?)

We're headed to Kenya later this summer and plan to stay for a few months, at least. Rafe wants me to get a better handle on that part of the estate if I'm to continue in my (now official!) role as second in command of the great Pembroke empire. I prefer to call myself Vice President Pembroke, especially when talking to humorless solicitors. Rafe pretends that this offends his dignity, but I know better. Luckily, I always find myself amusing.

Chantelle and I communicate only by text now, and it's lovely. We've never got on better. It's almost as if she's a real mother.

If you ask me about starting a family one more time, I will cut you off. Handbags at dawn, etc. I mean it. I don't care if you're a princess. Rafe and I have a few more demons to exorcise before we're ready to take that step, I think. We married in haste, have no plans to repent, but are easing into our future very, very carefully, even so.

But we'll get there, I promise. In our own sweet time.
Love,
Angel

MATTEO & IZZY...

From: izzy@santinapalace.org
To: allegra@santinapalace.org
Subject: Did you find my shoes?

I'm SO sorry I left without saying goodbye last night. I wasn't exactly planning on almost giving birth right in the middle of the Rock 'n' Royal concert—that wasn't part of my performance! I was trying to get to the VIP box to see you before I flew to the hospital. But Matteo said that although he's resigned to being married to an exhibitionist he drew the line at me giving birth on stage with a global audience of millions watching. LOL. At least I managed to finish singing before I went into labour and it gave him an excuse to be macho and show off his flying skills in an emergency.

Anyway, I took my shoes off backstage because my feet were killing me after all that prancing and gyrating and I wondered if you'd found them? I did text you but it was all a bit frantic and Matteo just didn't get why I was bothering with a pair of shoes when I was about to give birth. I told him they were my favourite Jimmy Choos and he just looked at me blankly, which just goes to show that men are from Mars and women are from Bloomingdale's. Please tell me you picked them up—they're the ones with the tiny bow that you borrowed for that charity thing you did with Alex?

And now we've got the important stuff out of the way (<gg>) I need to tell you that you're officially Aunty Allegra! Daisy Rose Alysson was born at 5:30 this morning and has been yelling ever since. Matteo thinks she has a louder voice than mine and is probably going to be an opera singer. Do you love the name? I'll tell you about it when I see you. It's a private thing between us (you know my favorite daisy necklace?) and I know the king is going to frown (doesn't he always?) because he'd rather we called her Arabella or something suitably regal, but we love it and Matteo loves her. I've never seen anyone so besotted. And guess what? I was in the birthing pool (sooo relaxing) and suddenly this song came into my head and I'm yelling at Matteo to get me a pen and paper because there's no way I wanted to forget it. Surreal.

Hope you enjoyed the concert. Matteo thinks it's going to raise more money this year than all the previous years put together. Still can't believe I was the headline act. All my dreams rolled into one. Thanks so much for coming. Hope you enjoyed the rest of it.

Tell me about you and come see me soon.

Love,

Iz

xxxx

RODRIGUEZ & CARLOTTA...

Sent from Rodriguez Anguiano's phone:

Rodriguez: Rescue me. Am at the mercy of Señora Garcia. She won't stop talking to me. And I think she wants to dance.

Carlotta: Aren't you going to oblige her?

Rodriguez: The last time I did that I barely escaped unscathed.

Carlotta: And who is it you're pretending to text right now?

Rodriguez: Someone very important. The Queen of Santa Christobel. That's you.

Carlotta: I'm aware! :)

Rodriguez: Aren't you going to rescue me?

Carlotta: As sexy as I find the idea of rescuing you, I'm far too busy. Eating lukewarm shrimp and enjoying the party. Where's your sense of fun?

Rodriguez: I left it back at home with the children.

Carlotta: It's not so bad to have a night out.

Rodriguez: Being at home in bed with my wife is a lot more fun than these stupid parties.

Carlotta: Your wife feels the same way. In fact, rumor has it she was spotted slipping out of the ballroom and is now waiting for you in the cabana by the beach.

Rodriguez: Really?

Carlotta: Really. I've been waiting for a while now, Rodriguez. Don't keep me waiting any longer.

Rodriguez: On my way. But you know this could cause quite the scandalous headline.

Carlotta: I'm always up for a little scandal with my husband.

LEO AND ANNA...

Dear Lucy,
Today you came into the world, and already I hardly know how I ever lived without you. We named you Lucinda, after my mother, but Lucy is more fitting right now. You are so very tiny for even that short name. I'm writing to you, baby girl, because I have so much to say and I'm not sure how good I'll be at saying it. But I want you to know that I'm going to try. Every day of your life, I'm going to try to be the best father I can be. I love you, sweetheart, more than I ever thought possible. You and your mother are everything to me. The smartest thing I've ever done was to insist your mother get into a plane with me after I met her.
Love always,
Daddy

Dear Lucy,
Your father has made me cry. Today he showed me this letter, and he told me he plans to write to you often, until one day you are big enough to read his letters. I think it is a marvelous idea. He also gave me a present today, to commemorate your birth. A small island. One day I will explain the significance of it to you, but not for many, many years yet. I have named it Lucy's Island. I think we will build a small cottage there and visit it from time to time. There is a beautiful shadowed cove with the bluest water you've ever seen. I can't wait to show it to you.
Love always,
Mummy

COMING NEXT MONTH from Harlequin Presents®
AVAILABLE DECEMBER 18, 2012

#3107 A RING TO SECURE HIS HEIR
Lynne Graham
Tycoon Alexius is on a mission to uncover office-cleaner Rosie Gray's secrets, but getting up close and personal has consequences!

#3108 THE RUTHLESS CALEB WILDE
The Wilde Brothers
Sandra Marton
When Caleb Wilde's night of unrivalled passion with Sage Dalton results in an unexpected gift, he stops at nothing to claim it!

#3109 BEHOLDEN TO THE THRONE
Empire of the Sands
Carol Marinelli
Outspoken nanny Amy Bannester may be suitable for Sheikh Emir's bed, but the rules of the crown forbid her to be his bride.

#3110 THE INCORRIGIBLE PLAYBOY
The Legendary Finn Brothers
Emma Darcy
Legendary billionaire Harry Finn is formidable in business and devastating in the bedroom. What he wants, he gets... Top of his list? Secretary Elizabeth Flippence!

#3111 BENEATH THE VEIL OF PARADISE
The Bryants: Powerful & Proud
Kate Hewitt
A passionate affair on a desert island wasn't top of Millie Lang's to-do list; but one look at Chase Bryant has her thinking again!

#3112 AT HIS MAJESTY'S REQUEST
The Call of Duty
Maisey Yates
Will tempting matchmaker Jessica agree to Prince Drakos's request? Share his bed before he takes a *suitable* wife?

You can find more information on upcoming Harlequin®
titles, free excerpts and more at www.Harlequin.com.

HPCNM1212

COMING NEXT MONTH from Harlequin Presents® EXTRA
AVAILABLE JANUARY 2, 2013

#229 SECRETS OF CASTILLO DEL ARCO
Bound by His Ring
Trish Morey
When Gabriella finds herself in alluring Raoul's gothic *castillo,* she knows the key to her lavish prison lies in succumbing to his touch!

#230 MARRIAGE BEHIND THE FACADE
Bound by His Ring
Lynn Raye Harris
It's not easy to divorce a sheikh! Sydney must spend forty nights in the desert—and Sheikh Malik will make sure it's more than worth it....

#231 KEEPING HER UP ALL NIGHT
Temptation on her Doorstep
Anna Cleary
Ex-ballerina Amber knows exactly where noise polluter Guy can put his guitar! But Guy knows a much more exciting use for her sharp tongue!

#232 THE DEVIL AND THE DEEP
Temptation on her Doorstep
Amy Andrews
Forget Johnny Depp...modern-day pirate Rick is pure physical perfection—and just the thing to cure author Stella's writer's block!

You can find more information on upcoming Harlequin®
titles, free excerpts and more at www.Harlequin.com.

HPECNM1212

REQUEST YOUR FREE BOOKS!

 Harlequin *Presents*

 PASSION · SEDUCTION GUARANTEED

2 FREE NOVELS PLUS
2 FREE GIFTS!

YES! Please send me 2 FREE Harlequin Presents® novels and my 2 FREE gifts (gifts are worth about $10). After receiving them, if I don't wish to receive any more books, I can return the shipping statement marked "cancel." If I don't cancel, I will receive 6 brand-new novels every month and be billed just $4.30 per book in the U.S. or $4.99 per book in Canada. That's a saving of at least 14% off the cover price! It's quite a bargain! Shipping and handling is just 50¢ per book in the U.S. and 75¢ per book in Canada.* I understand that accepting the 2 free books and gifts places me under no obligation to buy anything. I can always return a shipment and cancel at any time. Even if I never buy another book, the two free books and gifts are mine to keep forever.

106/306 HDN FERQ

Name _____ (PLEASE PRINT)

Address _____ Apt. #

City _____ State/Prov. _____ Zip/Postal Code

Signature (if under 18, a parent or guardian must sign)

Mail to the **Reader Service:**
IN U.S.A.: P.O. Box 1867, Buffalo, NY 14240-1867
IN CANADA: P.O. Box 609, Fort Erie, Ontario L2A 5X3

Not valid for current subscribers to Harlequin Presents books.

**Are you a current subscriber to Harlequin Presents books
and want to receive the larger-print edition?
Call 1-800-873-8635 or visit www.ReaderService.com.**

* Terms and prices subject to change without notice. Prices do not include applicable taxes. Sales tax applicable in N.Y. Canadian residents will be charged applicable taxes. Offer not valid in Quebec. This offer is limited to one order per household. All orders subject to credit approval. Credit or debit balances in a customer's account(s) may be offset by any other outstanding balance owed by or to the customer. Please allow 4 to 6 weeks for delivery. Offer available while quantities last.

Your Privacy—The Reader Service is committed to protecting your privacy. Our Privacy Policy is available online at www.ReaderService.com or upon request from the Reader Service.

We make a portion of our mailing list available to reputable third parties that offer products we believe may interest you. If you prefer that we not exchange your name with third parties, or if you wish to clarify or modify your communication preferences, please visit us at www.ReaderService.com/consumerchoice or write to us at Reader Service Preference Service, P.O. Box 9062, Buffalo, NY 14269. Include your complete name and address.

HP11B

It all starts
with a kiss